Five Deadly Words

Also by Keith Colquhoun:

The Money Tree (Hamish Hamilton)
Point of Stress (Hamish Hamilton)
The Sugar Coating (Chatto & Windus)
St Petersburg Rainbow (Chatto & Windus)
Goebbels & Gladys (John Murray and Academy Chicago)
Filthy Rich (John Murray and Academy Chicago)
Kiss of Life (John Murray)
Foreign Wars (John Murray)
Killing Stalin (Smaller Sky)
Beyond Reason (Solidus)

The Economist Book of Obituaries (with Ann Wroe)

Five Deadly Words

Keith Colquhoun

Copyright © Keith Colquhoun 2010
ISBN 978-1-904529-49-1

The right of Keith Colquhoun to be identified as the author of this work has been asserted in accordance with Sections 77 and 78 of the Copyright Designs and Patents Act 1988.

All characters in this publication are fictitious and any resemblance to real persons, living or dead, is purely coincidental.

All rights reserved.

No part of this publication may be reproduced, stored in a retrieval system, or transmitted, in any form or by any means, without the prior permission in writing of the publisher, nor be otherwise circulated in any form of binding or cover other than that in which it is published and without a similar condition including this condition being imposed on the subsequent purchaser.

A catalogue record for this book is available from the British Library.

Published by Solidus
www.soliduspress.com

For Grace, Toby, Jessie, Edward, Mary and Andrew

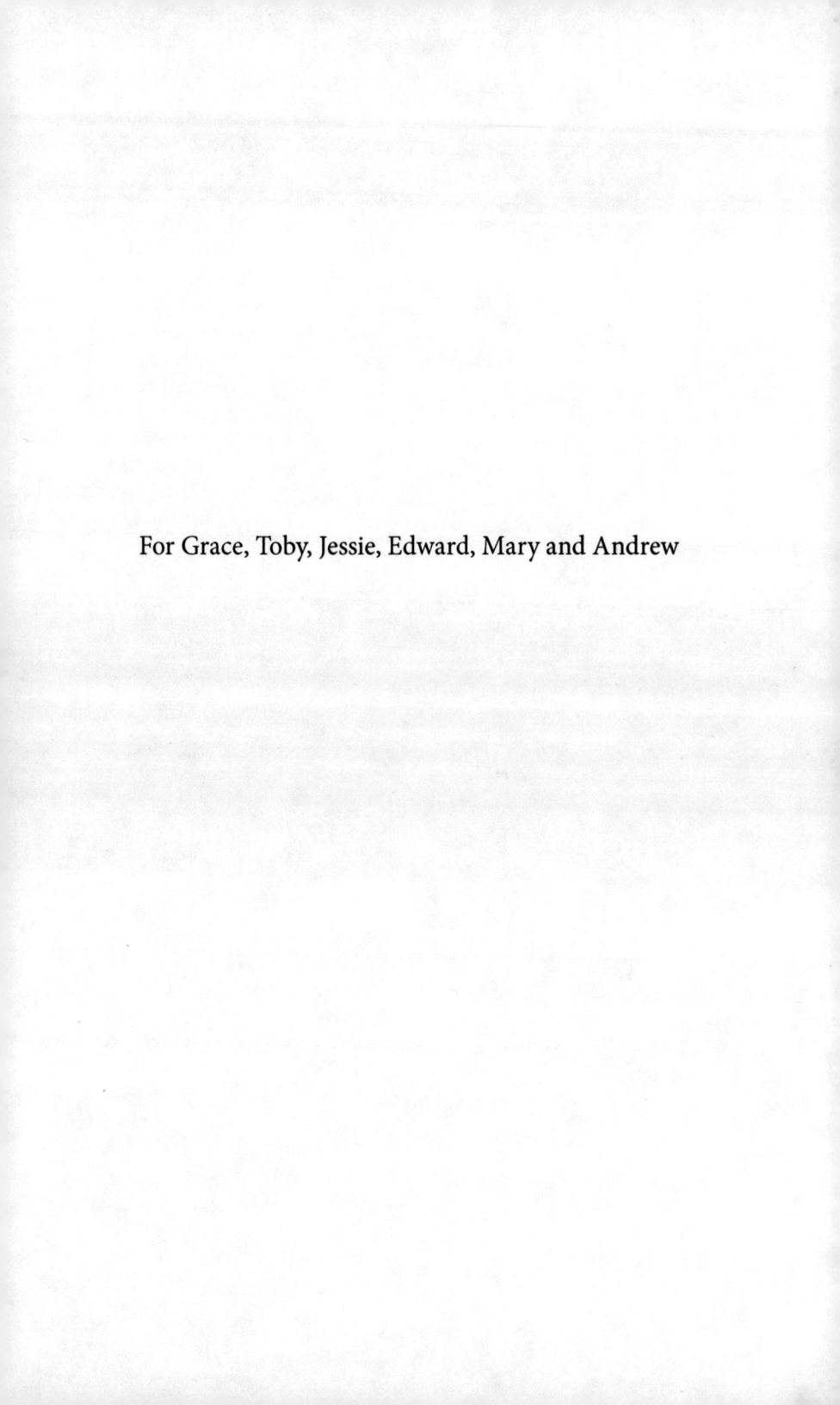

ONE

When Lucas began his exile in Britain he wrote to the Queen: 'My dear Elizabeth, I trust you are well. May I come to see you? It would be a solace to know that I had a sympathetic friend with whom I could recall happier occasions.'

One of the Queen's secretaries replied: 'Her Majesty commands me to thank you for your letter and to say that she is in good health. The Queen hopes your stay in this country will be a pleasant one. She is unable to grant you an appointment to see her.'

Lucas wrote to the prime minister: 'Relations between our countries have always been amiable. I should like to make use of the time I find I now have at my disposal to consider ways in which this relationship could be further strengthened. It would be helpful if, as a prologue to such considerations, we could meet. How about a working lunch?'

Next day he wrote to the foreign secretary: 'I am attaching a copy of a letter I wrote to the prime minister, whom I now understand from a newspaper report is out of the country. I should be honoured if you would accept my invitation instead.'

Three days later Lucas had a telephone call asking him to come to the Foreign Office. The young man who interviewed him there said, 'You've got to stop writing these stupid letters.'

'Is that the way you usually address a Head of State?'

'My message to you is that you are an embarrassment to Her Britannic Majesty's government.'

'I should like to speak to your superior.'

'No chance. And he's a lot ruder than I am.'

Lucas took his distressing experience of British diplomacy to the American Embassy. He had been an American protégé until he was deposed.

'Not surprised a bit,' said the man at the embassy who dealt with former protégés. 'Youngish fellow? Gucci loafers, yellow tie?'

'Australian accent.'

'A New Zealander. The Kiwis just don't care.'

'Should I complain?'

'If you must.'

'Will it do any good?'

'No.'

'Will you do it for me?'

'No.'

'You're talking like the Brits.'

'But politer.'

'Am I expected to be pleased?'

'Count your blessings. Count your money. Always a consolation, I'd have thought.' He smiled. Lucas did not smile back.

'I want some work to do.'

'Ah, work.'

The American selected a pipe from a rack on his desk, and sucked at it. He was not a smoker. He put his feet on his desk and gave an impression of thought. What sort of work did you find for a former dictator?

'A little lecturing, perhaps,' the American said. 'I have an aunt back home who runs a circuit. She might know someone here. Have to keep politics out of it, of course. Give us a sight of your notes. No reminiscences about dear Queen Elizabeth.' The American was already losing enthusiasm for the idea. 'What about some study? The Brits run a thing called the Open University.'

'Why don't I just read a good book?'

'Don't get shirty, Lucas.'

Lucas got up. 'Have a nice day.'

'Sure. Look, Lucas, let me think about this. Keep in touch.'

Lucas had already left the room. He returned to Claridges. The doorman saluted him as his car drew up. A signal went through the hotel so that a lift was waiting to take him to his suite. He waved the liftman aside and walked up the stairs. Anyone, however ordinary, could buy servility. Lucas hated feeling ordinary. He asked himself why he was living in a hotel. A president in exile should have something more established than a bed hired by the day. The following week he moved into an apartment in the district of central London known as St James's. This was one of the places in London that Lucas had heard of. While president, he had appointed a number of ambassadors to London and they had been accredited to the Court of St James.

'Is the court near here?' he asked the man from the estate agency who showed him the apartment.

'The court, sir?'

'Of St James.'

'I don't believe there is one, sir, as such.'

'No Court of St James?'

'I believe it is an historical concept.'

'It is where ambassadors present their credentials.'

'At Buckingham Palace, I believe, sir. You can see the roof of the palace from here. Beyond the trees. Heavenly view.' He waved in the direction of the sky.

'The court is really at the palace?'

'In a manner of speaking, sir.'

'How puzzling.'

'It is one of our funny ways, sir. Not uncharming when you think about it.'

The man from the estate agency was young, polite, neatly dressed and confident. He sold himself as ably as he sold his properties. He would be a guide in a new land.

'Would you like to work for me?'

'That's extremely flattering, sir.'

'You mean, no?'

'Perhaps you should not ask me, sir.'

So polite. Yet it was a rebuff, another humiliation, as complete as had been the rebuffs from the Queen, the Foreign Office and the Americans. He chided himself for having asked. But he missed having people around him. The entourage who had been glad to accompany him to safety in America had preferred to stay there when he moved on to Britain. He did not want to return to America, and America would probably not want him back. It did not warm towards losers. Where else to go? The world seemed puzzlingly small to a former dictator looking for a home. Latin America seemed eternally unstable. Africa was a sink. Australia was soft. Singapore was hard. Lucas had turned to mother Europe, with its antique ways and sublime tastes. Britain, the almost European country, offered an insular feeling of security. He was safe but he was bored, and he was snubbed. Creatures such as the serf at the Foreign Office, that lackey, that insect to be crushed, dared to treat him as a pariah.

Lucas told himself he would not forget. But he was an intelligent man. For the present at least, he was powerless. His American protectors had cynically withdrawn their support, preferring the upstart who had deposed him. Each day Lucas had lengthy phone calls to those few of his former lieutenants who had remained behind and who said they remained loyal to him. He told them how to deal with the new government, and, most important, how to sustain the morale of his supporters. How many in today's demonstration? Ten thousand. Possibly twenty thousand. What is 'possibly'? Who counted them?

It was a testing time for Lucas, trying to maintain his authority over several thousand miles through a satellite link that tended to fade and might be bugged by the enemy. For the first time in his career he had to assume that his underlings were trustworthy, although it was more than probable that they were not, exaggerating the amount of support for him, assuming that this was what he wanted to hear. Or they may have gone over to the enemy, paying their acceptance fee by playing the traitor to him. He longed to know what had happened to his palace, his home for years and from which he had to flee like a debtor escaping from a bailiff. But he could not bring himself to show weakness by asking for what might be called trivial information. And if the information were truthfully given it would be a penance to hear: of drawers rummaged and intimate letters read, wardrobes ransacked by souvenir hunters, the whole place put on show to the mob, even his grandchildren's toys. A family's life pried into and scoffed at.

By comparison, the troubles and responsibilities of Lucas's fellow countrymen in exile seemed minimal. There were in London, he had discovered, a surprising number of his countrymen and countrywomen. The word had got round that Lucas was in London too, and they came to see him. Some of their problems existed simply because they were abroad rather than at home. Most could be solved by the provision of an air ticket. Lucas usually directed them to their consulate but would occasionally, if he had been moved by a sad story, lend them the money. He never gave money away although he knew that the loans were unlikely to be returned. He could have transported the entire London community of his countrymen home in aeroplanes with mink-lined lavatories and hardly noticed the expense, but it would be a poor purchase. Only the frugal can seem to be generous. His advice tended to be earthly practical.

'But should we go home at all?'

'Of course you should.'

That was his answer to this question, always, to anyone, no matter who, no matter that they might be arrested the moment they arrived and jailed and maybe shot, perhaps deservedly, being agitators, thieves, murderers or miserable discontents. There was no other answer he could give. The questioners were either fools, in which case they were going to get into trouble anyway, whatever answer he gave, or they were provocateurs, hoping to get him to say something unpleasant which would be reported back with slobbering embellishments to his detested successor as president; and probably reported as well to the Brits, who would send him a polite but frigid letter reminding him that one of the conditions of his residence in the United Kingdom was that he should say nothing, on any subject, at any time, to anyone under any circumstances.

The passage of apparently harmless visitors to his apartment may have made Lucas unusually careless about security: that and the feeling that came from living in a part of London regarded as safe. After all, the Queen herself was a near neighbour. The attempt on his life therefore came as a shock to Lucas, most of the shock being that he, the former president of a notoriously unsafe country, had allowed his defences to slip.

When the would-be assassin arrived, Lucas questioned him briefly through the video-phone that connected his apartment to the entrance to the building.

'Courier, sir. Special delivery.'

The courier looked like one of Lucas's countrymen, which should have aroused Lucas's suspicion. A 'special delivery' from the new government would surely be connected with something sinister. A minute or two later the courier was at the front door of Lucas's apartment. He was holding a parcel, about the size of a shoe box. He handed it to Lucas. It had his name on it, dignified by the appellation 'His Eminence'.

'Where are you from?'

'Straight from the airport, sir.'

'I mean, your home.'

The courier named a village.

'When were you last there?'

'Yesterday, sir.'

'You must be tired. Come in for a moment. I'll give you something for your trouble.'

Lucas went to a bureau drawer to find a tip. Momentarily, his back was towards the courier. When Lucas turned, the courier was close behind him holding a gun.

The courier said, 'I'm sorry to have to do this, sir.'

TWO

The sequence of events in the next immeasurable moment is a matter for conjecture. What is certain is that Lucas kept cool and the courier did not.

'I can make you rich,' Lucas said, uttering the five deadly words that in his long career had frequently rescued him from difficulty.

The courier hesitated only for an instant, but it was enough. Lucas's right hand, instantly charged with the power of survival, crashed against the side of the courier's head, hurling him to the floor. The courier fired, dutiful to the end, but the bullet's mischief was only to destroy a lock in the bureau, although reducing its value a little should it ever come to auction. The adrenalin pumping into Lucas had him pouncing on the courier's gun and discharging it for the second time, this time decisively into the courier's brain.

Lucas's initial reaction was exultation. Survival is a very fine feeling. Although Lucas had been responsible for many deaths, this was the first time since he was quite a young man that he had killed face to face, in combat, and, moreover, with the odds stacked against him. Luck had been with him. He resolved to chide his astrologer who had told him he was entering a period of no danger. He flopped on to a sofa and waited for his pulse to slow down. What followed was, if anything, even more extraordinary.

A man had come into the room. He wore overalls and gloves.

'Get with it, Mac,' he said to Lucas. He went to the package the courier had brought and ripped it open. Inside, wrapped in transparent film, was something in green plastic. The man unfolded it and laid it along the floor and zipped it open. A body bag.

'Take the legs, Mac.'

Lucas told himself afterwards that he must have helped to move the body into the bag. He remembered that the body was already starting to stiffen. The bag was zipped up and the package left the flat on the man's shoulders. Lucas opened a french window and went out to the balcony. A small car moved away from the kerb and drove off at some speed.

The front door of the flat was still open. Lucas closed it. How did the intruder get in? Perhaps Lucas had left the door open when he had admitted the courier. What about the door at the entrance to the building, which had an electric lock? These questions, although puzzling, seemed minor compared to the mystery of the body snatcher. Presumably he had been instructed to collect a body. The only identification needed would be that it would be newly dead and in this flat. It was a flaw in what otherwise was a well-designed killing.

Handing Lucas the package containing the body bag intended for him was a macabre touch. Lucas recognised the body bag; at least, he was familiar with its type. After the Vietnam War, the Americans had a lot over which they gave away to friendly governments, Lucas's among them. A number of Lucas's enemies had ended up in American body bags.

Lucas contemplated his drawing room. Some blood had spilt on the carpet, but it had already dried and the carpet was red. It seemed unlikely that the woman who cleaned the apartment would notice it when she arrived for her duties the next morning. He put away the gun in a desk drawer. He regarded himself in a mirror and thought he looked younger.

THREE

Two days after Lucas's unfortunate experiences with British and American diplomacy, a Foreign Office official was on the phone to an American official he knew.

After an exchange of pleasantries the FO man said, 'This Lucas business?'

'He's been complaining?'

'He phoned the Palace.'

An American roll of laughter came down the line. 'Good for him. The Tower, the axe? Shall I send a wreath?'

'It's actually quite serious.'

'The Queen is displeased?'

'I'm displeased. The Palace is used to dealing with nuisances, but they are treated courteously. Lucas was told the complaint would be passed on.'

'Well, he was insulted.'

'Falkirk. Stupid bugger. But Lucas is more upset by the Americans. Dumped.'

'A little holiday. Do him good.'

'You'll have him back?'

'I'm not saying that.'

'He feels abandoned.'

'The heart bleeds.'

'He could be trouble,' the FO man said. 'Mischief. Boredom. Did we look after him properly? Questions might be asked.'

'Protect your back?'

'And yours.'

'I'm not sure I see this as a United States matter.'

'Lucas is your man.'

'Was. But isn't now. Britain is his host country. But look, let's not quibble. Keep a watch on Lucas. Point taken. Perhaps your police could help. They must have experts on this sort of thing. London is full of failed dictators. Let me ponder on it.'

The Foreign Office man put down the phone, feeling that Anglo-American solidarity was sometimes exaggerated. He spoke to the head of security at the Foreign Office, who said he was already overworked, but he offered the name of a detective at Scotland Yard that he thought looked after diplomatic matters. The detective said undiplomatically that he was surprised to get such a call at this time with the Brazilians making all this fuss about Stockwell.

'So you can't help?'

'They're your words.'

'Oh?'

'How much work is involved.?'

'Very little,' said the Foreign Office man, too eagerly.

'A nursemaid job?'

'If you put it like that.'

'For a day or two?'

A pause. 'Well, I suppose that would be a start.'

'I'm not promising you a top gun, but it's a sacrifice.'

'I'm grateful,' the Foreign Office man said, unwisely adding, 'let me know if there is anything we can do.'

'As a matter of fact there is. This Brazilian business…'

The sacrifice who was not a top gun arrived next morning.

'Mr Carruthers?'

'Smith. Carruthers Smith. My parents admired "The Riddle of the Sands"'

'Helen Berlin, nursemaid.'

'It wasn't my choice of expression.'

'No problem. I've been called worse things.'

Helen Berlin was, Carruthers judged, in her mid-twenties. Her hair was tidily bobbed. Her suit was neat. Her white silk blouse was almost prim. She spoke with confidence, like a BBC news presenter. Perhaps an educated copper.

'Well, sit down, Sergeant.'

'Not yet. Detective Constable.'

A constable. Carruthers wondered what knowledge Lucas might have of the hierarchy of the British police force. This might not have been a good idea. And now he had been landed with the Brazilian business. He left the room and returned with two coffees in plastic cups.

'How much have you been told about this job, Miss Berlin?'

'I'm to be Lucas's minder.'

Carruthers examined the word. 'Minder. Yes, in a way. Have you minded other people?'

'Yes.'

Carruthers waited for her to elaborate, but she said, 'I'm properly trained.'

'Sorry. Yes, I'm sure you are. I'm just feeling my way here. Been rather sudden. Lucas is a difficult customer. A bloody nuisance, not to mince words. But he is our guest. A responsibility. The good thing is, we don't think he is in any danger. I'm not sure we need to put a couple of tanks at his disposal.'

Carruthers smiled. Helen returned the smile, but only politely. It wasn't much of a joke.

'But you need to take precautions?' she said.

'That's it. Exactly.'

'I'm the precaution?'

'If you put it like that.'

'Some protection for yourself, if not for Lucas?'

Carruthers frowned. Had his request been so obvious?

'A little unfair, I think.'

'The case seems to be thickening, as we coppers say. You want to give Lucas protection without spelling it out?'

'As I say, a difficult customer.'

'Easily upset?'

'That's our experience.'

'Might blow his top if a slip of girl turned up as his minder? Not even a sergeant.'

'I'm not saying that.'

'I can take it, Mr Smith. We girls have to be tough as we prepare to take over the world.'

Helen Berlin, nursemaid and revolutionary, was considering what best to do. Her briefing, if it could be called that, was: *Toddle along to the Foreign Office, Helen, and see what they want. Don't take any nonsense. They seem to think we have nothing to do.*

Carruthers Smith's briefing had been even vaguer, as mindless as his name. What did he want? Nothing, except to say that he had done something. She could take her leave now. Write a report. There was always a report to write, even about nothing. It might even be read. *'Bloody FO. Bunch of layabouts. Now, Helen, have a look at this...'*

'Well, I'll keep in touch,' Helen said. 'Thanks for the coffee.'

But Smith was hesitating.

'I hoped you might stay around a bit. You could look at Lucas's file. His letter to the Queen might amuse you.'

Helen stayed the rest of the day. Smith took her on a tour of the Foreign Office. She affected to be unimpressed by the architecture, designed to intimidate any foreigner with the might of the British Empire, but she paused over the portraits of foreign secretaries stretching back to antiquity. One was of a woman. Her tenure had been brief.

'It is rather a male bastion,' Smith said.

'They fear a woman would pull it down?'

Smith grunted. 'Ernie's your man.'

He pointed to a photograph labelled 'Ernest Bevin, 1945-1950'.

'He wanted to demolish it?'

'So it is said. Replace it with a council house, like the one he was born in.'

Helen contemplated the picture. 'A foreign secretary called Ernie can't be all bad.'

'A matter of taste, I suppose.'

Smith seemed to have become bored with his role as guide.

'Must catch up with some work, I suppose. Has to be done today. Let me show you the Lucas bumf.'

The bumf consisted of half a dozen over-full folders. It looked less like an official dossier than ephemera of some celebrity collected by a doting fan.

Helen removed one of the folders. An earwig crawled out and quickly returned to the darkness within. 'I fear we are disturbing a nature reserve, Mr Smith.'

'There's good stuff there,' Smith said. 'Good stuff,' he repeated, more firmly.

Helen laid out the good stuff on a desk that Smith said belonged to someone who was away in Uzbekistan. Smith left to catch up with some work that he said had to be done today. Helen tried the drawers of the desk. One was locked, though it did not look secure. The others were unlocked and disclosed the detritus of a family man: some holiday snaps and an out of date railway season ticket to the suburb of Coulsdon. Underneath some papers was a packet that had contained a condom, of a type, the packet noted, that was ribbed and increased sensation. Helen wondered why a family man should bring a condom to work, and what had happened to the condom. Had it been put to use in the workplace of Palmeston and Ernest Bevin? Were ribbed condoms that increased sensation routinely used in Coulsdon, and if so why had the empty packet turned up, partly concealed, in the desk of the expert on Uzbekistan?

Helen gently pulled at the locked drawer. It would probably yield to a hairpin, but perhaps not now. Perhaps never. She would be patient. She turned to the folders. She looked briefly at the decaying newspaper clippings, much holed where earwigs had dined. She read the letter that Lucas had sent to the Queen, and a number of other letters that Lucas had sent to various dignitaries who had befriended him when he was in power, but were not friendly now. She leaned back in her chair.

Through a window she could see Horse Guards' Parade, bereft of horses and guards but with a sight almost as strange, a man in a bowler hat, perhaps an escaped diplomat, and beyond that St James's Park where prime ministers used to walk along the lake and put their minds from politics. Beyond that, though out of sight, was Green Park. Lucas had a flat overlooking Green Park. Helen had noted the address on the letters Lucas had sent to unfriendly former friends. She thought she had had enough of this awesome building for the moment. She would follow the prime ministers' example and view the lake and its exotic birds. She might even go as far as Green Park, not to see Lucas, of course not, but to, what? sense his environment, to use a fashionable word. It would be a sensible thing for her to do.

Helen followed the prime ministers' path along the lake. A pelican was trying to kill a pigeon. Perhaps the walk had not taken their minds off politics after all. She walked on towards the bridge over the lake where the sparrows are so tame they will take food from your hand. She had no food, but thought the sparrows looked plump enough. It was decision time. She could walk across the bridge towards St James's tube station, she could return to the Foreign Office or she could push on to Green Park. The tube station had an exhibition of old posters; interesting, but she had seen them before. She was not yet pining for the Foreign Office. Green Park selected itself. She saluted Buckingham Palace as she crossed Birdcage Walk. The royal standard was flying, so presumably the Queen was at home today. She wondered if Lucas could see the palace from his flat. Probably he could, although there might be trees in the way. She sat on a park bench from which she thought she could view Lucas's balcony, although she was not sure. Lucas's was probably the one to the left with a palm tree just visible. There was no balcony to the right. A few minutes later Helen was outside Lucas's front door. She realised, because she tried to be honest with herself, that it had been her intention to call on Lucas from the moment she had decided to go for a walk.

Probably she was exceeding her duty. But she felt brave.

FOUR

Smith had not encouraged her to call on Lucas, but nor had he told her not to. It was reasonable to assume that Lucas would be pleased to meet the person who had been assigned to protect him.

She would not know that Lucas had become particularly wary of callers. He assumed that the people who had sent the killer would realise their mistake and return with another bag, this time to fill it with the correct body. But nothing untoward had happened and after a few days Lucas was able to relax a little, and he put down the incident to bungling by a government of bunglers. Even so, he reacted with caution when a television company telephoned requesting an interview. They wished to do a programme about his country and would be grateful for guidance. Lucas knew about television. At home he had kept it under a firm hand. But he had seen enough of British television to know that it was disrespectful. Seeking 'guidance' sounded like a not very subtle ploy to get access to him, and he said no.

When the bell rang at the entrance to the building Lucas examined the entry-screen for a full half minute. It was possible that the television people had turned up anyway. However, there was no television crew hovering, just an unaccompanied young woman.

'Yes?'
'Helen Berlin, Foreign Office.'
'Are you expected?'

'I was hoping to speak to Mr President.'

It was a long time since Lucas had heard those graceful words.

'Please come in, Miss Berlin. In the lift press the button marked Penthouse.'

Before Lucas opened his front door he examined Helen through the spyhole. Presentable young women can carry guns.

'You have identification?' he said, with the door half open.

Helen produced her police identity card, which bore her name and her photograph but did not state her rank.

Lucas took the card, waved Helen into the hall and then into the sitting room. He stood by a window and examined the card with care before handing it back.

'You are from Scotland?'

'New Scotland Yard. It is the name of a police headquarters in London.'

'You are from the police?'

'Attached to the Foreign Office, Mr President.'

'You know who I am?'

'Famous people do not need identity cards.'

'Well, sit down, Miss Berlin, and tell me your business. Let me have your coat. I expect you find it warm in here. I am not yet used to the famous English climate.'

Helen sat and said her rehearsed piece: 'It is the aim of the Foreign Office to provide security to important guests to our country. Sometimes the FO calls on the expertise of the police.'

'You think I am insecure?'

'We hope you are not. But we offer a service.'

'A sentry at the door?'

'Perhaps nothing so dramatic. The royal parks have their own police. They should have been told to keep an eye on your place. I will check. We can send an expert to see whether your flat is secure and make recommendations if it is not. Windows, access and that sort of thing.'

'Is this a new policy by the Foreign Office?'

Helen smiled. 'Hardly. Nothing new about the FO. Proper fuddy-duddy of a place.'

'Apart from the security matters, do you have any message for me?'

'I don't think so. Well, welcome to Britain. But I expect you have heard that already.'

'I have to tell you, Miss Berlin, that I had a very unwelcoming encounter at the Foreign Office. And all because of a letter I wrote to your esteemed Queen. A courteous letter. Most courteous.'

It was, Helen thought, an unobjectionable letter, the one she had seen. But Lucas had written many letters, and some idiot at the Foreign Office had lost his temper and abused Lucas. Should she apologise?

'I blame myself,' Lucas said surprisingly. 'I had met your Queen before in happier circumstances. When I came to England I presumed too much. I saw us, God forbid, as equals. Coming from Sulu, a republic and a democracy, that was my way. But I am old enough to remember when Sulu had a queen and people would prostrate themselves in her presence, yes, flat on the floor. Queens are divine. Your Queen was right to reject me.'

Helen was unsure how to respond. The Queen a divine? Sulu a democracy? She thought she would leave quite soon. She had done what she has set out to do, to see what a dictator looked like, albeit a retired one. Mission accomplished. She stood. 'Well, duty calls.'

'Nonsense, Miss Berlin. It is the teatime hour. Taking tea, I have heard, is the English duty.'

As though on cue, tea arrived on a large trolley trundled in by an elderly Asian woman. It was unfashionably comprehensive. A teapot and a tray of biscuits, the normal components for afternoon tea, were merely the framework around which were arranged carbohydrates in many forms. The servant disappeared. Lucas looked towards his guest.

'Shall I?' she said.

'Lemon, please, Miss Berlin. No sugar.'

She handed Lucas his tea, and a plate. 'What shall I pass you?'

'A biscuit would be very nice. Thank you.'

'All this, and you ask for a biscuit?'

'I'm glad you are pleased. It is a pleasant occasion, the English tea. Now please, as you say, tuck in.' He watched as Helen passed over the currant bread and the dish of strawberry jam, and took a muffin. 'I fear you are going to disappoint me.'

'Fear, disappoint. You are a bit extravagant, sir.' Lucas noted that she had dropped 'Mr President'. Still, 'sir' showed respect. He watched her survey the flat with its huge sitting room and its promise of other huge rooms; not so much a flat as a portion of a vast house that had been cut up into large slices, leaving some over to be wasted, as most of the big and expensive cake on the trolley would be wasted.

'Extravagant. You talk like my enemies,' Lucas said.

Lucas saw her eyes flicker momentarily, but she did not follow up with an obvious question. .

'Tell me about Sulu,' she said.

'You tell me what you know, and I will try to fill in the gaps.'

'I know it is in Asia, not much more. Somewhere north of Borneo.'

'It is a start, more than most people know about it.'

'Unhealthy?'

'It is too hot, and there is malaria and other diseases that people die of, though not so many die since I built a hospital.'

Between Lucas and Helen Berlin was a coffee table on which there was a coffee-table book. Lucas opened it and turned the book towards Helen.

'The hospital?'

'Correct.'

Lucas reached forward and turned the pages, commenting as he did so. He had built this building. The Americans had paid for this one. Was it, perhaps, a little vulgar? Lucas lingered over each page. Helen noted that he was not yet half way through the book. He seemed reluctant to let her go.

He shut the book. 'I am boring you.'

'Not at all,' Helen said, not very convincingly.

Lucas got up and walked to a window. After a few moments he said, 'Come here, Miss Berlin.'

Helen contemplated the expensive view. Yes, you could see the palace. But Lucas directed her attention to a woman who was walking on the terrace of a nearby house.

'What do you think?' Lucas said. 'Something particular about her?'

There was a routine to her walk, not unlike that of the sentries who paced the pavement outside St James's Palace nearby. Lucas took a set of binoculars from a bureau drawer and examined the woman through them. He handed the glasses to Helen.

'You note she is of Levantine colouring, a little Arab slave.'

Helen peered briefly though the glasses, then handed them back to Lucas.

'You know her?'

'Almost I feel I do. Every day she takes her exercise on this little terrace, getting a little fresh air from the confines of her room. The slaves of London. Locked away in these big houses. It could happen to anyone. Anyone, Miss Berlin.'

'Are you trying to alarm me?'

'I thought she might be of interest. More than my silly book. You are a police officer.'

'It all sounds very dramatic. But a woman walking up and down on a balcony? I'm not sure even Beckett could make something of that.'

'Not waiting for Godot, perhaps, but who is she waiting for?'

Helen smiled wryly at Lucas's turning of her snobbish remark. 'You think she has been abducted?'

'Live and let live. A Christian police officer might not understand the ways of Islam.'

'Either this woman is there against her will, or it is all in your imagination, Mr Lucas. If she is a prisoner, she should be freed.'

Helen was aware that a tension had entered their conversation.

'What is will, Miss Berlin? We are all prisoners of some kind. She seems to be well treated.'

'But this is Britain.'

'Oh, Miss Berlin. I expected better of you.'

'This isn't Sulu.'

'I understand your flag waving. But I put this to you, because I believe you have intelligence. Captivity may be the natural condition of man. Free countries may simply be on parole. Every society may be a captive society, allowing freedom only to those who do not endanger it.'

'Philosophical words.'

'You flatter me.'

A buzzer sounded. Lucas picked up a telephone.

'Yes? Oh yes.'

He replaced the telephone.

'Miss Berlin, I apologise, but I have to leave you, just for a few moments.' He pointed to the book on the coffee table. 'Do feel free to browse.'

Helen opened the boring book that seemed to have disturbed the atmosphere. When Lucas did not return immediately she did a circuit of the huge room. She thought better on her feet. She paused at the window. The prisoner, if she was a prisoner, had left her terrace. Helen sliced a wafer of chocolate cake from the over-laden trolley. She loved chocolate. She looked at her watch. Eleven minutes had passed since Lucas had left her alone. She surveyed the room. The largest piece of furniture was a desk. Its lock looked as though it had been freshly damaged. How odd. She opened a drawer. Inside was a gun. Every dictator should have one. It was a semi-automatic, a compact instrument of violence in a tasteful shade of green. Two bullets were missing from the magazine. Perhaps fired. Helen sniffed the barrel.

Perhaps recently. She replaced the gun and closed the drawer. She examined the smashed lock. The damage could have been caused by a bullet. Possibly. How odd. She looked at her watch. Lucas was taking his time. Twenty minutes passed, and now Helen was feeling cross. She wondered what to do. Another five minutes went by. She decided to leave. Ladies should not be kept waiting, even by former dictators.

The door through which she had entered the room was locked. She tried the door through which Lucas had left the room. That was locked. This was absurd. She banged with her fists first on one door and then on the other. They were solid, unyielding, not at all like the doors you bought at your local DIY store. Helen flopped on to a sofa. She had to think. The phone. She lifted the receiver. Dead. Of course. Her mobile phone. But that was in the pocket of her coat, which the courteous Lucas had taken from her. Think then. It was possible that the doors had been locked by accident, perhaps by some electronic switch that had flipped. It was possible that at the same time the phone had broken down. It was possible that Lucas had been whisked away to deal with some totally unforeseen emergency. All possibilities, but so improbable as to be dismissed without further consideration. Lucas had made her a prisoner.

FIVE

'My dear Miss Berlin, this is terrible. What can you think of me?'

'Some problem, Mr Lucas?'

Helen closed the book she had quickly picked up from the coffee table as soon as she heard Lucas opening the door. She looked at her watch.

'Goodness, it is getting late. You must have had urgent business, Mr Lucas?'

'You must forgive me.'

'Absolution is granted.'

Helen smiled briefly and held Lucas's eyes. Did the shit really believe that she had hardly noticed his absence for nearly an hour? It did not matter. What mattered was that she had kept cool.

'Is there anything more I can do for you, Miss Berlin?'

'You've done more than enough, Mr Lucas. The chocolate cake was delicious. I took the liberty of helping myself.'

Lucas had her coat in his hands. As she put it on she said, 'I will check that the park police will keep you in mind.'

'I hope you will too, Miss Berlin. I am always happy to have another philosophical discussion.'

After leaving Lucas Helen Berlin walked from Green Park though Milkmaids Passage, into St James's Street and along Pall Mall as far as the Royal Automobile Club. Her father had arranged for her membership of the club, which she regarded as far too stuffy for her own taste. He said it would be a refuge from what he believed was the rough world of the police. Its redeeming asset for Helen was its pool. At this time in the afternoon, before the suits arrived at the end of their working day, the pool was almost empty. Helen slid into its cool grasp and began to relax. The encounter with Lucas had taken a lot out of her. Being locked up was one thing; having to control what she regarded as her naturally healthy temper was worse. Lucas had no doubt expected to be confronted by an angry woman when he at last reappeared, in tears perhaps. Helen had steeled herself into a state of calm. She sank her head and moved into a crawl. After six vigorous lengths she was herself again.

When she was dressed she felt into her coat for her mobile. She had better let the office know she was still on duty. There was something else in the pocket. Something knobbly in the corner. She fished it out. A black bead, the size of a child's marble. How odd. Helen was sure it had not been there earlier. Surely she would have noticed it when slipping her mobile into her pocket. But why would Lucas have given her a bead, if it was a bead? Did it have some sinister Asian meaning 'Beware, or the spirit of the bead will haunt you.' Helen had an imagination.

SIX

Helen Berlin was in the office of her boss at Scotland Yard. His name was Jenkins and he held the rank of superintendent, roughly equivalent to being a middle manager in civilian life. He was wearing a white shirt with blue stripes. One of the stripes was not quite regular. It had suffered a cigarette burn which Mrs Jenkins had had invisibly mended. His wife had said that the craft of invisible mending was clearly not what it was, like so many things, but Jenkins was surprised that it still existed, albeit in a more visible form, rather than having been dispatched by the disposable society. He doubted whether Helen Berlin wore anything that had been mended, invisibly or otherwise. Whenever he saw her, her clothes looked as though they were new that day, to be replaced next day with a new lot straight from the shop. Her newness made him feel his oldness. He assumed that he had reached the limits of his career as a policeman. His value now was as a reservoir of experience available to the young and clever that the Yard saw as its future. Helen Berlin could soon be a sergeant, then an inspector. In a few years she could be a superintendent, a title that had taken Jenkins thirty-two years to achieve. And beyond that, what? Perhaps even a commander.

Now, what was she talking about? Yes, the Lucas affair. She wanted advice. That was a reasonable request. Who else could she go to? Santa Claus?

'You believe he may have killed someone?'

'Some violence happened in that flat, that's all I'm saying. Just conjecture.'

'Lucas locked you up?'

'I couldn't get out of the room. He apologised. It might not have been intentional.'

'But you were worried?'

'A bit. Of course.'

Nasty character by all accounts. It probably wasn't a good idea to send Helen Berlin to see him. Bloody Foreign Office. When Jenkins first became a policeman the force was mostly dealing with what were called ordinary decent criminals, or ODCs. It now seemed strange that not all that time ago a burglar might be 'nabbed' and surrender peaceably because it was a 'fair cop, guv'. British movies at the time had got it about right, through they seem improbably comical now. The ODCs belonged to an era when top footballers were paid one hundred pounds a week and people stood when the national anthem was played. While Jenkins routinely deplored the emergence of a new generation of criminals who carried knives and guns and were often high on drugs, he had to concede that they made police work more interesting. Commendations he had received for improving police strategy in dealing with the thugs, including some for personal bravery, had helped him to gain promotion. But what Helen was talking about was different. Of course it was different, but different in a way that disturbed Jenkins. He did not find it interesting, in the way that he had found violence interesting. You knew where you were with violence. It was nasty, but it was simple. This was politics. Politics was not simple.

Jenkins said, 'Shall I give you a rest from this business?'

'I'm to be sacked?'

'Come off it, Helen. I'm trying to help. Take a breather.'

'Who would take over?'

'I'm torn between a detachment of Guards from the Palace or some Special Forces just back from Afghanistan; but things being what they are, Lucas will have to be satisfied with Hobbs.'

'I like Peter. He's always been decent to me.'

'Well, there you are. It shows where decency gets you. Hobbs should be able to handle Lucas's little ways.'

'And I can't?'

Jenkins saw the way the conversation was going and suddenly felt weary. Was Hobbs a better bet because he was male? That was the feeblest of arguments in what Jenkins supposed might be called the post-feminist era.

'He has experience,' Jenkins said.

A strong argument, he thought. Hobbs had been a member of many teams of minders assigned to protect foreign visitors. Too many probably, but he was never likely to be promoted to a more demanding job, Minding sounded tough, even dangerous, but it was one of the softer numbers of police work. Ex-dictators were usually grateful for sanctuary. They did not usually make prisoners of police officers.

'Give me another day,' Helen said.

'To do what?'

'Salvage my pride. Round things off. Write a report.'

Jenkins was shaking his head, slowly. He did everything slowly. Then he said, 'Keep your report tight then. Just the facts. No conjecture.'

'Thank you, sir.'

'But I don't want you back in that flat.'

'No, sir.'

'Better report direct to me.'

'I will, sir.'

As she left his office he called, 'Helen, don't do anything stupid.'

She left the Yard and walked to her club in Pall Mall and had a swim. Seven lengths. An extra one for confidence. Jenkins's decision to take her off the Lucas case had been a shock.

There was a text message on her mobile. 'WHERE R U? JB.' Helen was inclined to ignore it. Joel Butcher could be overwhelming. She wanted to think. She phoned the agent who had let the flat to Lucas. He confirmed that the desk was in good condition when Lucas had moved in. Pristine, he had said. Who fired the shot that damaged the desk? Presumably not Lucas. Why would he fire at his own desk? More likely, someone had fired at him. Perhaps twice: two shots had been fired from the gun, if in fact that was the weapon that had been used. No conjecture, Jenkins had said. But all crime involved conjecture, and that was only a posh word for guesswork. Helen sent a message to Butcher. She wanted to have the company of someone almost normal.

SEVEN

'You know what it is, of course?' Butcher said.

Helen had shown him the bead that was in her pocket after she left Lucas.

'Clearly I don't.'

'It is black, as you noted with your usual perspicacity. Well, not quite black. There's a subtle touch of grey that gives depth to a decent pearl.' Butcher, Joel Butcher, rolled the pearl between his fingers in the manner of a television expert showing off in the Antiques Roadshow. They were drinking coffee in the upstairs lounge of the club. Helen, neat except for a strand of wet hair from her swim that had strayed across her forehead; Butcher, large and sprawling in jeans and leather jacket.

'From Tahiti, I'd assume,' Butcher said.

'Now you are making it up. You are probably making all of it up.'

'How suspicious you are, Helen. Black pearls do not grow naturally. Dye has to be inserted in the poor oyster. It's what they do in Tahiti these days instead of posing for Gauguin. When you get back to your office, look it up in a book. I presume you police people have books?'

Helen said nothing. This was stay-cool day.

'I suppose you did some holiday programme about Tahiti?'

Butcher smiled. 'I'm rumbled again. But it wasn't a holiday piece and it wasn't specifically about Tahiti. It was about deceptions in jewellery. Quite serious.'

'Quite serious.' Helen repeated the phrase flatly, suppressing a temptation to be sarcastic. Butcher made television documentaries and he wanted to do one on Helen entitled, provisionally, *A New Type of Copper*. Helen had laughed at the proposal, and it still made her smile when she thought of it. If there was one thing that could stymie her career in the police it would be her portrayal on television as the brilliant antidote to a force run by Officer Plod. As it was, she was resented by many of her colleagues for her law degree and for being marked out for rapid promotion, and probably for a lot of other things, including a preference for espresso coffee. She had made plain to Butcher her reasons for saying no and he said he respected them and would like to remain a friend. 'Respected' though was not the same as 'accepted' and she suspected that Butcher had not abandoned his absurd plan. Still, she enjoyed his company. At the age of twenty-four Helen Berlin was still considering with whom she would be prepared to spend the rest of her life. Butcher was not her lover, but he was a possible candidate. But only possible. Perhaps five out of ten. He was easy to talk to. Perhaps too easy. How much had she told him about her visit to Lucas? Probably too much.

'Is Lucas trying to compromise you?'

'Why would he do that?'

'Don't underrate Lucas.'

'I don't. I never underrate people who lock me up.'

'He's a sadist?'

'Possibly.'

'What other reason?'

'Perhaps he was bored. He must find life tedious after being a dictator. But I'll have to think about it. It may be more complicated. Supposing he left me alone, guessing that I would poke around the room? Perhaps he was watching me through some hidden camera, looking though his desk, finding the gun and the damaged woodwork?'

'I'm worried about you, Helen.'

'That's nice.' Butcher went up to six out of ten.

'Seriously. This madman, firing off guns, threatening to make you a slave. He should be in jail. Should he have a gun at all?'

'I don't suppose he has a licence.'

'Then he should be arrested. He's breaking the law.'

'You can't arrest people just for breaking the law, or everyone would be in jail. I'm probably breaking the law, sitting here with you, wasting taxpayers' money, when I should be catching burglars or making motorists' lives difficult.'

'You are an odd copper.'

'So I am told. Frequently.'

'How did the exam go?'

'It went.'

'You passed?'

'I haven't been told. Police secret.'

Helen had recently taken the first part of an exam to be promoted to sergeant.

'Sounds bad, eh Helen? Failed, and so young. This conspiracy to destroy the careers of our best and brightest. Don't worry, Helen. Your voice will be heard. Your face will be seen. Scotland Yard will slink back to Scotland.'

A waitress appeared to offer more coffee, interrupting the conversation, and Butcher lost interest in his sally. He still held the pearl.

'Shall I take charge of it?'

Helen reached over and took the pearl from Butcher. 'You leave my pearl alone. It's not every day that a girl is so nicely compromised.'

'I too come bearing gifts,' Butcher said.

'Oh dear. It sounds as though you want something from me'

'How suspicious you are, Helen. No, as always I am thinking of your career.'

'Out with it, then.'

Butcher felt into a side pocket of his jacket, pulled out a crumpled piece of paper, smoothed it out and handed it to Helen. It was an advertisement torn from a newspaper. It was headed 'Great opportunity'. Helen gave the details underneath not more than a glance.

'What are you up to, Butcher?'

'There you are, Helen. Someone tries to do you a good turn and gets nothing but a slap round the kisser. Disheartening, really. Now read the advert properly.'

Helen read the small print. 'The money, I suppose you mean? Must be a misprint.'

'It has appeared elsewhere, all with whacking great pay.'

Helen examined the advertisement again. 'What am I supposed to do about it?'

'Say thank you, perhaps.'

'Come on, you're never your best when being mysterious.'

'Read it again.'

There was something in the advertisement that seemed, not exactly familiar, but she felt should be familiar. Helen was beginning to feel irritated.

'The telephone number,' Butcher said at last. 'I called it. Lucas's.'

Yes, Helen thought, she should have recognised it. It was on Lucas's notepaper. The last two digits were Helen's age. Butcher was good at finding things.

'How strange,' she said.

'I thought you'd be interested.'

'Strange that I didn't spot it. I must be slipping. "An Idiot Type of Copper". That should be your programme.'

'Oh?' Butcher seemed to be considering the idea.

'Don't be ridiculous.'

'Did I say anything?'

'I know what you are thinking. Constable Berlin is not totally brain dead.'

Butcher said, 'What about dinner tonight?'

'Thanks, but I'm already being wooed. But thanks.' Seven out of ten. Well, perhaps six and a half.

'You're too good for him.'

'Who?'

'Anyone.'

'Oh, shucks.'

'I mean it. What's he got?'

'Nice clothes, for one thing.'

'Nicer than mine?'

'Honestly, I can't understand why they let you in here.'

'Sheer personality.'

'You always say that.'

'It's always true.'

Helen was still holding the advertisement.

'Does he bring you interesting clues?'

Helen looked at the scrap of newspaper. It meant nothing, but she put it in her purse.

EIGHT

The restaurant need not be identified except to say that it was quite famous in the silly way that fame is accorded to minor accomplishments. French cuisine, of course. Tonight, as on most nights, it would be full. But it was not yet eight o'clock and only three tables were occupied.

At one table were a couple, obviously American, who had dined early and were almost at the end of their meal. They would be leaving soon, having added a sizeable debit to the man's charge card account, but perhaps having learnt the valuable lesson that if you wished to savour the atmosphere of a posh restaurant when it was busy you should not eat early. At a table in a corner were two women who had just arrived. One of them wrote about restaurants for a newspaper. She claimed that she never revealed her identity. But the manager of the restaurant recognised her from the photograph that appeared with her articles. He wondered whether to greet her, but decided not to, at least for the present. He had, however, spoken to the cook. She should not be poisoned, despite her strange calling as a food critic.

At the other occupied table a man sat alone. He looked to be in his mid-thirties. He was reading a book. The restaurant did not entertain many book readers, although newspapers and magazines were occasionally seen at the dinner tables. The eccentricity was noted by the staff and commented upon. One of the waiters thought the man might be famous, that he had seen his picture somewhere, perhaps even on television. From time to time quite well-known people ate at this restaurant. The name in which he had reserved his table, David Robinson, told the waiter nothing, but it could be an alias; David Robinson sounded like an alias. On reflection, though, the waiter thought it unlikely he was famous. He did not look famous. He thought the face might be familiar because the man could have been to the restaurant before, although not recently, and not with a book. It was the book that had drawn attention to Robinson. When his guest arrived it was assumed that he would put the book aside and behave like a normal customer. He had complied with convention to the extent of ordering a pre-dinner drink, a whisky with water, which he sipped occasionally as he read.

His guest arrived. Robinson showed a vestige of surprise at her appearance. Helen Berlin had spent a lot of time on her face, embalming it, getting her skin to a shade that she later told David she called Garbo white. She had on a long black coat and what looked like a French priest's hat. David watched a waiter greet her and offer to take her coat. She hesitated briefly, then allowed him to remove it. He pointed to the hat, and she handed that over too. Helen, the fearless detective, did not feel entirely at ease. The Home Counties middle classes, for all their airs, believed in frugality. This restaurant was clearly not an expression of frugality and David probably could not afford it. However, he was no doubt thinking of the meal as an investment. Helen was fond of him. She was unsure how the evening would end, but she would try not to be unkind. In her lexicon of possible suitors David rated eight, or a possible nine, out of ten.

The waiter pushed a chair under her bottom and smiled professionally. He was good at his work; he made people feel relaxed. He deserved the fifteen per cent service charge that would be added to the bill, assuming that it would be passed to him. Restaurants like their guests to dress up, and the effort Helen had made to disguise her natural appearance was probably no more extraordinary than the effort the restaurant made to disguise the food it served.

David closed his book and put it first on the table, and then on the floor. He got up slowly, almost reluctant to abandon the composure he felt up to a few moments ago, with his book and his watered whisky, within the calm folds of the almost empty restaurant. He seemed momentarily uncertain how to greet his guest, but she offered a white cheek.

'Do I look all right?'

'Exactly right, Helen.'

Helen was wearing what on a man would be called a dinner jacket, although the material looked thinner and softer than a man would choose, and the bow-tie was casually floppy. The waiter asked her if she would like a drink and suggested one. The name meant nothing to Helen, but she nodded in agreement.

'I must be late.'

'I was very early.'

'What are you reading?'

David picked up the book and showed Helen the spine. It was something about old ships. David Robinson was a historian.

After a few such commonplace exchanges composure returned. Helen was at ease. She had drunk her drink, which was something red in what looked like a medicine glass, and she now examined the menu. The couple assumed the identity of conventional diners. Helen's white face was unexceptional in the dimmed light. The dinner-jacket dress looked attractively ambiguous. It had received the approval of David's penis, which had stirred like an old dog that sensed it might be more interesting to be awake than asleep.

'I'm very hungry,' Helen said.

Seduction suddenly seemed less possible. Anyone preparing to eat extravagantly was not usually expecting passion afterwards. Perhaps, David thought, he had made a misjudgment. 'Feel free,' he said. He would die like a gentleman.

'You're sure?'

'Never more so.'

The restaurant offered a treat for the greedy called Menu Rabelais, consisting of seven courses. None of the courses was itself large, but seven, David thought, would make a tight fit in the stomach. This was Helen's choice.

When the waiter had departed with instructions for a feast David seemed a little gloomy. Helen did not mind gloomy men. They gave the impression of reliability, although there had to be a balance. David was not, she knew, gloomy all the time. Often he was amusing. She wondered if he was gloomy about what she had ordered. She reached across the table and touched his hand. 'This is really nice,' she said, adding, softly, 'Darling.' Helen was not by nature a darling person, but David seemed to need consoling.

The restaurant was filling with people who gave the impression that they were closely familiar with the place, that they were entering a room of their own. They did not need a waiter's tact to make them feel comfortable. He was accorded a nod, called by his first name, and then forgotten. At a table near to Helen a woman had arrived dressed in a cutaway hound's-tooth jacket, a black divided skirt with hemline frills that could be seen just below the white linen tablecloth. She wore a small bowler beneath which was a fuzz of Eton-cropped hair. 'Ambiguity must be the taste of the moment,' Helen said. David regarded the woman for several seconds, then returned his attention to Helen.

'You look adorable,' he said. 'I love the brooch.'

The 'brooch' was the black pearl she had found in her pocket. Helen had resolved to return it immediately to Lucas, but her resolution had been undermined when, on impulse, she had gone into a jeweller's in Bond Street where she had once helped to investigate a break-in. It was, said their pearl man, an exceptionally fine specimen, quite remarkable. He clipped it into a silver mounting to show its glow. This was the brooch Helen was wearing.

'From Tahiti,' Helen said. 'They grow them there specially.'

'Grow them?'

'Black pearls don't grow naturally. Dye has to be put in the oyster.' Helen recycled her recently acquired knowledge with an air of scholarship. She did not believe in attributions.

'You do know an awful lot, Helen.'

Helen acknowledged the compliment with a modest shrug. David was decent, trustworthy, a warm human being. This might well be his night. She said, 'Does the name Lucas mean anything to you?'

David took a sip of water. 'Of course. Brave man. Tried to shield Nelson when the sharpshooters opened up, then carried him below. Hardy got all the publicity though.'

Helen told him of the more recent Lucas. David showed interest and she told him of her visit to Lucas's flat. David asked some intelligent questions and she told him some more. He did not express the concern for her safety that Butcher had done, but Helen suspected anyway that Butcher's concerns had been insincere.

'It's a nice little mystery,' David said. 'You believe someone was killed in the flat?'

If someone had been killed, Helen thought, what should she do about it? What could she do about it? Jenkins had warned her off. She was expected to be a good girl, write an innocuous report and return to the Yard for some 'real work.'

Helen's reverie was broken by the arrival of the wine, and then the food. The plates were covered with metal domes like Prussian helmets, which the waiters doffed with a flourish. Helen ate the succession of dishes placed before her with gannet-like swiftness.

'These snack things are jolly good,' she said.

Helen was the nice little mystery, David thought. That was her attraction. Everyone had a bit of mystery about them and that was, at least at first, what you were attracted to, might fall in love with. If David were married to her she would discard her pose, perhaps quite quickly. Two breakfasts together and it would be gone and be replaced by something, not unpleasant, but without the mystery. David had been married. His wife had died four months ago, and he missed her.

Helen was examining the menu, presumably for a filling pudding. But, as if somehow sensing the drift of his thought, she said,

'Cancer is a nasty beast.'

'It was TB, not that it matters.'

Helen returned the menu to the waiter and gave her order.

'How very unusual,' she said to David. .

'It's getting less common.'

'That's how Garbo died.'

'Is she dead?'

'In "Camille".'

'I don't think I've seen it.'

'I've got a video if you want to borrow it.'

'Perhaps when I need cheering up.'

'You need another wife, but I expect you know that. I say it as an adviser, not a contender.'

'Do you know of any, going cheap?'

David had intended it as a joke, if a feeble one, but Helen did not smile. She seemed to be considering it as an option. She said, 'You must make an honest appraisal of what you have to offer, and try to attract someone who can offer at least as much, more if possible.'

'Market forces.' David said.

'Sorry?'

'It's what economists talk about.'

'It is a bit like finding a new job.'

'What about love?'

'Love is sex,' Helen said. 'Of course, part of the package.'

David said nothing. Helen did not like silences. 'Think of your first marriage as an apprenticeship,' she said. 'Your second will be different, might be better. The third may be different in another way. You can trade up all the time.'

'Is that what you believe?'

'I like the sound of it. Might change my mind tomorrow.'

'Lettie used to say we were designed for each other.'

Helen was not in a sentimental mood. She said that she had read about a Paris brothel of the 1930s. When a customer arrived the madam would call out, 'Choosing time, girls', and the girls would form a tableau from which the customer would make his choice.

'If half a dozen women appeared before you now, not tarts, upmarket women if you like, you could make a choice, and probably live with her as well as anyone. Most of the best women are married, or committed. You have to go head-hunting. Try a few out. Must be difficult, poor David. Can't seal it off?'

David experienced a slight shock, although not an unpleasant one. The possibility reappeared of bed with Helen. Perhaps the quite extraordinary amount of food she had eaten had not entirely quelled her passion. Perhaps she digested food unusually rapidly.

Helen rested her spoon on its plate and leant across the table and touched David's hand. He wondered if she was going to offer an endearment, but she said, 'Do you think the funds would run to another of these delicious puddings?'

The chef himself brought Helen's second pudding to the table. Perhaps he wanted to see for himself this considerable container of his handiwork. The chef and Helen exchanged a few inconsequent remarks. When he left Helen said, 'A charming man.'

'Charming?'

'He took an interest. It was a lovely compliment.'

For Helen it was decision time. Her companion needed to know if his investment was going to yield a dividend. The wifeless David would have many millions of little fish between his legs longing to be released. At least that was her assumption. For all she knew, he paid for sex three times a day before meals.

Helen had met David at a publisher's party. She had looked in for fifteen minutes to give support to a friend who had a book out, and had found David so interesting that she had stayed for two hours. They had not talked about sex. His obsession was the unpromising one of Nelson, but his enthusiasm was attractive. He had suggested dinner, when lunch would have been safer. Helen touched David's hand again. 'You've been lovely and charming too. You have a gleam in your eye, as my mother called it, and perhaps something hard in your pocket. This is good for your future. Women like to be observed.'

David leaned across the table towards her. She thought for a moment that ardour had overcome decorum and that he was reaching for her breasts. But a morsel of pudding had splashed her pearl brooch, and David was dabbing it with his napkin.

Helen took the napkin from him. 'Silly me. Oh dear.' She frowned, but the frown was not for the spilled pudding. The pearl: what should she do about that? Lucas's generous gift. A loose end.

'Something wrong?'

'The pearl. I suppose I have to return it.'

'It seems an innocent gift.'

'Nothing's innocent at the Yard. I'm sure there's a memo about taking gifts, even innocent ones. Probably a book of memos.'

'Play safe then.'

She would, she thought, like to keep the pearl. But it would be stupid to do so. Play safe. David was right, again.

'He will be difficult. Probably lock me up again. Anyway, I'm banned from the flat.'

'The mail? First class. No, perhaps not.' A pause. 'You need a courier.'

'Would you, David? You really are a good friend.'

'I have never met a dictator. Nelson, though, was very authoritarian.'

A waiter was at the table. He had a compendium of cigars. David shook his head. As the waiter moved away Helen caught his arm. She took out a cigar, sniffed it and listened to its soft crackle.

'May I, madam?'

She handed the cigar to the waiter for the end to be cut. Her father had taught her how a cigar should be prepared. She took the cigar into her mouth and sucked gently at the flame offered by the waiter. A pause, then she blew a perfect smoke ring across the table towards David. Gently, she put a finger through the ring.

'What would you like to do now?'

NINE

Helen was in Jenkins' office. He was reading something and waved her to a chair without looking up.

Eventually he said, 'Clever little thing.' He pointed to the document he had been reading. 'You've seen this?'

'No, sir.'

But she had seen enough from a glance at his desk that it was the results of the sergeant's exam. The exam, lasting several hours, was a series of multiple choice questions, mainly on law. She had not found it difficult and estimated that she must have exceeded the pass mark of fifty-five percent. Clever little thing? Patronising, but praise was praise.

Jenkins passed the document to Helen. Her mark was ninety-seven percent, the top mark of the two hundred or so who had sat for the exam. She returned the document to Jenkins. 'I must have made one mistake. I wonder what it was.'

Jenkins exploded with laughter. 'You're a character, Helen. You really are.'

A clever little thing and a character, all in one day. Where would it end?

'Now, Helen, this is just a start,' Jenkins said, himself again. 'No sitting on your laurels. You realise that? Part two, the practical part. The important part, in my view. Not a sergeant yet, eh? I'm a busy man, but I'm going to help you, push you if need be.'

'Thank you, sir.'

'Now you need a schedule of work. What are you doing now?'

Helen handed Jenkins an envelope containing the report she had written, no conjecture, just the facts.

Jenkins looked at the envelope, but did not open it. 'Yes, Lucas. Blasted man.' He slapped the envelope on the desk.

Helen said nothing. Jenkins was thinking. Helen felt she could guess his thoughts. Hobbs was to take over. An end to her first solo job. Disappointing, but she wouldn't grumble. Police work was not for prima donnas.

But Helen's guess was wrong. Hobbs was suddenly busy. He was part of the team minding the Olympic torch as it proceeded through London. 'Minding the Chinese minders, that's the problem,' Jenkins said. 'Blasted thugs. Sorry, Helen. I'll have to leave Lucas with you for a bit longer.' He slapped the envelope again. 'Nothing here to worry me, I take it?'

'Just stuff for the record, sir.'

'Good. We shouldn't have taken him on. Foreign Office. Pain in the arse, excuse my French. Do what you can to wrap it up.'

'As soon as I can, sir.'

As she left the room he called out, 'Well done.'

She supposed she had made Jenkins happy, briefly. She supposed she should be happy herself. Almost a sergeant. But what about Lucas, brooding, bored, impulsive, a gunman? Well, a gun owner, almost certainly a gun user. Wrap it up, Jenkins said. Wrap what up? Stupid phrase. Lucas was a danger to the peace of the community. A good phrase. She should have been frank with Jenkins, not sheltering in a cocoon of praise. A sudden thought: David Robinson. She needed to talk to him about the foolish errand she had sent him on. She called his number. No response. Any normal person, she thought, she could get on her mobile. But Robinson was the only person in Britain who did not have a mobile phone.

TEN

St James's is not a large district. David Robinson, should he wish, could walk across it from, say, Piccadilly to the gates of Buckingham Palace in fifteen minutes at a brisk pace. Even if he dawdled, looking in a shop window, Lobb's say, with its extraordinary boots for ladies, the trajectory would take no more than half an hour. Yet Robinson never felt confined by the area. On the contrary, to leave it was to be reminded of its quality. Just trespassing beyond Piccadilly Circus he felt he was in the native quarter, while to the north there was the vulgarity of the Bond Street shops, and beyond them the bazaars of Oxford Street. South of the river was all third world. St James's was an island, like Holy Island in the Dark Ages, a defence against barbarities, against the casual use of foul language, against plays in which nothing happened, painting in which nothing was painted, against muggers, traffic fumes, of nearly everything.

Robinson wanted to live in St James's. But telephone an agent whose board advertises a flat for sale, and a woman with a posh voice will mention a price that will test your composure. Nevertheless, Robinson told himself that the district contained a variety of people of modest means. St James's Palace, the nicely-preserved ruin at the bottom of St James's Street, was where loyal lackeys lived in quarters kindly lent to them by the Queen. The decently-small brass plates on the doors advertised the tenants, Colonel This, Sir Something That. They asked for nothing sumptuous, just a respectable address and the right to have fresh flowers every day. In Bury Street, not far away, there were modest shops with living quarters above the premises. That is to say, they looked like shops: they had shop windows within which were old-fashioned paintings presumably for sale. But they were the unbusiest shops in the world, each presided over by an English midinette in a pleated skirt and blouse who spent her day reading, though discreetly. Robinson had sometimes walked slowly, and covetously, down Bury Street, contemplating the premises with their rooms above. No doubt shopkeepers lived in some of these rooms, but some might be empty, and the owner might be glad to have someone who would be there at night, and would not be unwilling to keep an informal eye on things, listening for possible intruders, that sort of thing,

Robinson entered a shop. The midinette slid her book into a drawer and offered him a smile, not warm but not unwelcoming, She assumed that Robinson was not going to buy anything. He did not look rich and stupid, the two characteristics she associated with buyers. He might be someone who had lost his way and wanted directions to Piccadilly. She looked at his shoes. They were commonplace shoes, not the sort hand-made in Jermyn Street. She thought he might be a scholar; not a bad guess.

'Just browsing,' Robinson said in answer to an unasked question.

'Of course. Anything special?'

Anything special? It was like being in a barber's chair. He did have something he could talk about . One of the pictures on view was of a warship in Napoleonic times. He had noticed it when he stopped to look in the window. It was the reason why he impulsively chose this shop rather than another, or none.

'This one caught my eye.'

The girl stood, smoothed her skirt and stood by Robinson, bowing her head slightly in acknowledgement of the picture.

'Condy certainly knew his ships,' she said.

Robinson smiled and nodded. He had no idea who Condy was, whether he had some superior knowledge of ships not shared by other artists, or whether, as was probably the case, he was a hack who drew as well as he could as fast as he could. But it was not a bad remark, although presumably one that the girl frequently used as it was infinitely adaptable. Herring knew his horses. Van Whatsisname knew his flowers. Rubens knew his nudes. Would she say that? However, there appeared to be no nudes in the shop, by Rubens or anyone else. Ships, nothing but ships.

The girl said, 'There are some more Condys upstairs.'

Upstairs? Robinson ascended to the rooms that from the road seemed empty. The walls were dense with pictures. The girl pointed out three that she said were by Condy. They were smaller than the ones downstairs but otherwise identical. They could be photo copies of each other.

'Stuck to his subject, did Mr Condy,' Robinson said.

The girl frowned. Was she entertaining a sceptic? Art dealing was based on credibility. There was room for penniless scholars as well as moneyed idiots, but the scholars were expected to be respectful.

'We are expecting a lot from him,' the girl said. She spoke of Condy as though he were her promising contemporary instead of a forgotten name in ancient catalogues. Robinson thought of a flippancy, but discarded it. He sensed a trace of hostility from the guardian of the Condys. He had supposedly come into the shop to ask if there were a few spare rooms where he would be glad to act as watchdog. The plan now seemed absurd. He had been compromised by his imagination. How would he begin? 'By the way...'

Then she said, 'Are ships your subject?' The remark was almost personal. Perhaps he had misread her attitude.

'That period,' he said nodding towards a picture of a warship that looked about to sink.

'Ah, a historian. Should I know you?'

The girl did not look as though she had read Robinson on Gunnery.

'Just one book,' he said. 'Very specialised. Sea battles in Nelson's time.'

'Patrick O'Brian?'

'Aubrey and Maturin?' Robinson said.

'I've read every one.'

They returned to the ground floor. The conversation was pleasantly breaking free from formality. Robinson too had read O'Brian's sea stories; although not all of them as the girl said she had. She had voluntarily proposed a subject of mutual interest. That was quite flattering. Might she fancy him? Flirtation seemed an inappropriate activity in these rather sombre surroundings, and it was possible that he was misjudging what might be the girl's simple politeness. The long-married and now widowed David Robinson was out of practice with flirtation. He had been mildly perturbed when Helen had said, *try a few out*, although by then they had both drunk a fair amount of wine.

The girl was awaiting a response, but whatever Robinson was going to say was cut short when the street door opened.

'Good morning, Mr Voster,' the girl said.

Clearly, a known customer, perhaps a moneyed idiot.

'I'd better be pushing off,' Robinson said.

'Don't forget to sign our book,' the girl said.

Robinson inscribed his name and gave his former Oxford college as his address. He wondered if he should ask the girl for her name or whether that would embarrass her in front of her customer. However, she had a business card ready, with the name of the shop printed on one side and her name, Felicity Brogan, and a telephone number written on the reverse.

'Please come again, Mr Robinson, when you have time. There are some other very fine Condys I'd like you to see. You'll be hearing a lot more of Condy.'

That was not unsatisfactory, Robinson judged. Better than he could have hoped for. A door had been opened, figuratively. He wondered what lay beyond the first floor. Yet more pictures, perhaps, but equally possibly the upper rooms could be empty and lonely and waiting for occupation. With a feeling of optimism Robinson left Bury Street, crossed St James's Street and headed for the residence of the dictator of Green Park. The previous day he had phoned Lucas, who had not seemed surprised by Robinson's proposed visit.

'You work for Miss Berlin?'

'A friend,' Robinson said.

'I see,' Lucas said, obscurely. 'Eleven o'clock. Be on time.' On time. Certainly not late, but not early either. Dictator language.

Lucas met him at the door to his apartment, waved him in to the sitting room, then picked up a phone that was off its cradle. He had presumably been in the middle of a call.

Helen's vivid description of the room made it seem familiar. There was the desk wounded by a bullet. There were the doors she had pounded when Lucas had locked her up. There were the binoculars though which she had observed the slave on the balcony. There was the coffee table book with its boring pictures of Sulu. One of the doors opened and there was the woman pushing the trolley that had contained the extravagant tea, but was less laden this time. Robinson could smell coffee. Lucas, still on the phone, nodded in the direction of the trolley. Robinson laid out two cups and filled them with coffee. He pointed to the sugar bowl and Lucas nodded. At least with sign language they were getting on marvellously.

Lucas's caller seemed to be questioning him persistently. 'Yes,' Lucas said. 'No. No. Yes, certainly. No, not a misprint. That is the salary. Many applicants, of course. I'd like you to write me a letter. No, you must decide. I will give you an address to write to. Do you have a pencil, Miss…' The address Lucas provided was not the Green Park one.

'A thousand apologies, Mr Robinson.'

One would have done, Robinson thought, or none. Anyone could be held up by a telephone call. Lucas made even an apology sound sinister.

Lucas did not look apologetic. He seemed rather pleased with himself.

'How is Miss Berlin today?'

'Very sad, sir, at having to return your generous gift. They have this rule in the police about no presents. Silly, but there it is.'

Robinson produce a brown envelope with 'official' stamped on it.

Lucas opened the envelope and removed the pearl, which, Robinson thought, looked nothing special without its silver mounting. Even so, he experienced a sense of shock when Lucas took the pearl to the fireplace, put it on the hearth and crunched it under the heel of his shoe. He continued crunching it for perhaps half a minute as though it were some live thing that was attempting to escape.

ELEVEN

Lucas sipped his coffee and made a face. 'It is a peculiar feature of coffee,' he said, 'that it quickly gets cold. Tea retains its heat. An English quality, perhaps, eh, Mr Robinson?'

Carefully he placed his cup and saucer on the table next to the book on Sulu. It seemed that no revenge was to be taken on the crockery as it had on the pearl, if indeed revenge was Lucas's motive for putting it to death. Lucas had offered no explanation for crushing the pearl. What seemed to Robinson an eternity had elapsed since Lucas had returned to the sofa, but apart from his debatable observation about the relative heat-retaining qualities of coffee and tea, he had said nothing. Silences did not necessarily have to be filled up. But Robinson could not just sit there when something strange had happened. Helen had been locked up. Robinson had witnessed an episode of violence, albeit a minor one. Was Lucas mad? He was looking at Robinson intently. Was he expecting some response to his question about the English and tea?

'You seem an intelligent man, Mr Robinson, and I believe a trustworthy one. I can confide to you that I have not yet become accustomed to English ways. Miss Berlin declined the pearl. She was correct to do so. How foolish of me to place it secretly in her pocket. What must she have thought? Such honesty is uncommon among the ladies of Sulu, but not it seems among the ladies of England.'

Helen was all set to keep the pearl, Robinson thought, but was afraid of being found out.

'But why did you destroy it?' Robinson heard himself saying.

'Anger, Mr Robinson. Sheer anger. With myself. For belittling myself. Do you never get angry, Mr Robinson?'

Of course he did, like anyone else. But not enough to destroy things. . Robinson wondered how much a black pearl was worth. Hundreds? He had no idea. The jeweller Helen had shown it to said it was a good one. What on earth was Helen going to say now?

Fresh coffee had arrived, although Robinson could not recall Lucas ordering more. Again he laid out the cups and serviced them.

'Yes, much better,' Lucas said with a smile to Robinson, as though he had personally brewed the coffee. 'You can assure Miss Berlin that she will be rewarded.'

'She does not want a reward, sir. That is what she has asked me to tell you.' Best to make that plain, even at the risk of another outburst.

'That I understand. We have dealt with that, Mr Robinson. No stupid little gifts. But there are other rewards. There is friendship. Will you tell that to Miss Berlin?'

Did Helen want to be the dictator's friend? Hardly.

'I think she would want to keep her relationship strictly official, sir. Perhaps co-operation would be the word. Very necessary in making arrangements for the safety of a guest to this country.' What rubbish was he talking? But he had to say something.

'You are close to Miss Berlin?'

Close? A tricky word. No one could be closer. Did Lucas mean that? It was getting difficult to judge what Lucas meant about anything.

'I take an interest in her work, naturally.'

'As a historian?'

How did Lucas know that?

'She has a wide range of interests, the excellent Miss Berlin, even to naval gunnery?'

Robinson tried not to look surprised.

'You are too modest, Mr Robinson. You are famous. Robinson on Gunnery. I have a copy myself.' Lucas went to a drawer in the desk. How extraordinary, Robinson thought, he is going to produce one. And so he did, with the flourish of a conjuror.

It looked almost new, but that, Robinson suspected, was the condition of most copies. His publisher had been evasive about the number printed, but Robinson assumed that it was no more than 500. About 100 had been sent out optimistically for review. Sales so far were about 200.

He had telephoned Lucas only the previous day. It was possible that Lucas took an interest in seventeenth-century naval warfare, but not likely. Robinson guessed that out of curiosity Lucas had taken a long shot on the internet. Robinson had a website, but with depressingly few hits. The real surprise was that Lucas had obtained a copy of the book so quickly. A plus for dictators.

Robinson stood. It was time to extract himself from the dictator's lair. He walked to the window. The slave's balcony was empty. A sudden breeze was combing the pastures of Green Park. The grass had been allowed to grow quite long, perhaps, Robinson thought, because every blade had the value of an orchid.

'St James's is a pleasant district,' Lucas said, standing behind Robinson and sharing the view, 'but for most people, I fear, too expensive.'

For the first time Robinson felt, not apprehensive about Lucas, but irritated with him. Of course it was expensive, criminally expensive. Only criminals such as Lucas could afford to live there. Idiots such as Robinson had to fantasise about getting a free flat in Bury Street.

'A statement of the obvious, if I may say so. With respect.'

'My dear Robinson, my apologies. No offence was intended.' Robinson felt what was presumably a reassuring hand on his shoulder.

'Sorry. It's a raw subject.'

'Why not? You are young and want to make something of your life. It is not unreasonable to want to live in a pleasant district. But if I may take the risk of again stating the obvious, you will not get to live in St James's as a result of the royalties from your little book.' Lucas paused, stagily. 'Still, it is a book, on decent paper, published by a respectable firm, though I suspect not a prosperous one. It has had I believe one review in a respectable but not very prosperous publication, People are impressed, perhaps misguidedly, by books, even little ones. Are you writing anything else?'

'A book on Nelson.'

'Another little book?'

'Not so little.'

Robinson was planning a major reassessment of Nelson, arguing that Britain's greatest sea hero was a pathological killer. It was a stupendous task that Robinson believed would make his name. Whenever he considered it, which was often, he was surprised by his audacity, taking on a British god.

'What do you live on, Mr Robinson?'

It was an extraordinarily personal question. What was he to say? Bugger off? Perhaps not that. He was supposed to be Helen's emissary, and emissaries were not given licence to swear, even to dictators. He had been a teacher until his wife had died and he supposed he still was. The school had been sympathetic, but would now be wondering what would be a reasonable period for bereavement. Several times he had been on the point of writing to say he would not be returning, but the simple need for a salary had deterred him. Is this what Lucas wanted to know? Perhaps he knew it already. He seemed to know a lot about him.

'I manage.'

'I am sure you do, Mr Robinson. And my inquiry was not designed to intrude. I am trying to be helpful. Nelson sounds like several years of work.'

Was Lucas going to offer him money? He hoped not.

'What a writer needs is a patron,' Lucas said.

Robinson would not be rude. He would decline any offer gracefully.

'The best patrons are in America,' Lucas said. 'That is where you should look.'

Oh. Robinson experienced a tinge of disappointment. It would have been interesting to hear what Lucas would have come up with. Robinson moved away from the window. The door beckoned. But Lucas had not finished.

'I am not a medical doctor, as you may know. I hold an honorary doctorate of law conferred by an American university during a visit to Washington. It was a number of valentines pressed on me, for in those days I was regarded in America as freedom's beacon east of Malacca. This free gift of scholarship has, for a gift, been remarkably useful. In Asia having a doctorate, even an honorary one, marks one out as an esteemed being. Even in Britain, where only physicians attain that state of grace, I have been reluctant to shed this accolade, although I have to correct anyone who assumes I am a medical doctor. During my flight to Britain I had to disabuse a stewardess who asked me to attend a passenger suspected of having a heart attack, although I could have done what the real doctor did when one was found, loosening the woman's clothing and diagnosing indigestion, and would have done it more sympathetically. Doctoring is usually no more than a grinding patience and the application of simple nursing skills, perhaps not that, for many problems of the consulting room are not strictly medical.'

Lucas liked to talk, Robinson thought. Perhaps he was lonely. Perhaps it was a weakness. What was he getting at with all this doctor stuff?

Lucas offered him his hand. 'We'll leave it like that, shall we, Mr Robinson? I'll talk to my friends in America.'

'About what?'

Lucas smiled and gripped Robinson's arm. 'You writers.' Another squeeze. 'What I'll want is a synopsis of your Nelson book. It need not be long, just compelling.' When Robinson did not immediately answer, Lucas said, 'If not for you, consider this a little compensation to Miss Berlin for sacrificing her pearl.' A pause. Lucas went to his desk and opened yet another drawer and handed Robinson a large white envelope with Helen's name on it, written in silver and ornamented with scrolls. 'If you would be so kind.'

Later that day Robinson handed over the envelope to Helen. It contained a card edged in gold. It read, 'Madame and Doctor the Honourable F.S.K. Lucas request the gracious company of Miss Helen Berlin on March 3rd to commemorate Liberation Day, 6.30-8.30 pm.'

Helen tore the card in two, then placed the two halves together and tore them into four. She tried to tear them again but the bundle resisted her efforts and the pieces fell to the floor; face down, Robinson observed, except for one fragment that bore the words *gracious co...*

TWELVE

An invitation Lucas had sent to the American Embassy inviting a representative, or representatives, to his party on Liberation Day had not been accepted, indeed not acknowledged. He phoned the embassy to ask if the invitation had perhaps been mislaid and was told by a functionary that he would investigate and call back. After no one called back Lucas wrote to the Russian ambassador in London, inviting him to lunch. Since the collapse of the Soviet Union, the Americans no longer regarded Russia, the Soviets' chief component, as a serious competitor to the domination of the world. All the same, Russia remained a nuclear power and a possible enemy. The Americans, Lucas reasoned, would at least frown on his approach. They might even give some attention to their former beacon of freedom in Sulu.

The ambassador's secretary telephoned to say that the ambassador would be charmed to accept the invitation but that unfortunately his diary was full for the immediate future. Please accept his apologies, but would Dr Lucas find time to have lunch, or dinner, with one of the ambassador's most trusted deputies? Lucas accepted the diplomatic pretence that there was a long waiting list to eat with the ambassador, like a never-ending queue outside a Moscow store, and invited the valued deputy to breakfast. Over his second helping of scrambled egg the Russian invited Lucas for a trip to Moscow. Lucas said that, circumstances permitting, he would be delighted to go. That meant, as the

Russian fully understood, that he would think about it if the Americans persisted in shunning him. A visit to Moscow would be a journey from which, metaphorically, there would be no return. Lucas might do no more than gawk at the Lenin dummy and lose his way in the Rossia hotel, but the Americans would regard it as desertion, as surely as if he put on another uniform. They would strip him of his rank, of his medals, of his credit cards, rip away his epaulettes, defrock him, submit him to a body search and frame him with disinformation. Probably already they were upset that he had entertained the guzzling Russian to breakfast.

But if they were upset they were not showing it. So Lucas took to lunch a journalist from a posh paper who had once enjoyed his hospitality when he was president. The restaurant was an expensive one, regularly used by hawkers of doubtful information who added to the menu a propaganda course of their own. Along with his sticky pudding the journalist swallowed the item that Lucas had prepared for him. The newspaper then printed a story, an exclusive one naturally, that Russia, in its new post-Soviet expansionist mood, was 'making tempting overtures' to the ex-president who had consistently been a stalwart friend of the West. The article demanded to know if the Americans still had a firm grip on this strategically vital area. The cold war might be formally over but there was still a chill in the world. The communists had not gone away, only changed their name.

Lucas assumed that even if the Americans had missed the scrambled eggs, they would surely get this message from the sticky pudding. He was correct. An official from the American embassy phoned him.

'How are you, doctor?' A warm glow emanated from the earpiece.

'I am extremely well.'

'And Mrs Lucas?'

'She, too, is in the best of health.'

'The ambassador thought I should call you. Keep in touch, that sort of thing.'

'I was the tiniest bit disappointed that no reply has been received to my Liberation Day reception. Important in our calendar.'

'No reply?'

'None.'

'Well, that looks bad, doctor.'

'We were quite upset.'

'No one contacted you?'

'No one.'

'Hold on, will you, doctor?'

Dead air for a few moments, then the American said, 'Your invitation was most certainly received. It was ungracious of us not to come back to you.'

The pantomime over, Lucas waited to see what was on offer.

'Let me be straight with you, doctor. Looks like you've been rattling the railings a bit.'

'What does that mean?'

'Making things difficult, as the Brits say. Chatting to the Russians.'

'Are they not our allies? Did I not see a picture of Bush and Putin together? Smiling?'

'We are still pretty fussy about who we call our allies. But we may have been at fault ourselves here, doctor. Perhaps we should have done more to keep in touch with you.'

The long desired invitation was at hand. Lucas waited patiently. Would it be dinner or lunch? Dinner with the ambassador would be the prize. Breakfast with a lowly official would be a disappointment.

'How about a drink, doctor?'

A drink?

'We could touch glasses,' the American said. 'On an informal basis.'

Perhaps Lucas's feeling of let-down came through the telephone line, for the American said, 'Don't push us, doctor. It might be the start of something.'

At least the American wanted him to say yes. It mattered to him. He wasn't saying, take it or leave it.

'A drink would be very pleasant,' Lucas said.

When Lucas arrived at the Ritz, there were half a dozen people in the bar by the lobby. None of them looked like an American on a sensitive diplomatic mission. Lucas sat at a table and watched people come though the revolving door dressed in their smart clothes of admission.

'Can I get you something, sir?'

Lucas felt no desire for alcohol, and his stomach sought more than a glass of Perrier water.

'Would it be a great trouble if I asked for a glass of milk?'

'Milk, sir?'

'And a cheese sandwich. I suddenly feel hungry.'

'That looks good,' the American said when he arrived. 'I guess I'll have the same. I didn't know you could order milk.'

'Order anything. That's the reassurance you pay for.'

'Do you have goat's milk?' the American asked the waiter.

'I will inquire of the barman, sir.'

The American was even younger than Lucas had expected. He had the appearance of a bright teenager, but presumably he had been to college so would be in his early twenties. Lucas asked him if he had been in London long.

'Two years.'

'Ah.'

Berlin before that. Five years, six. And before that in Japan.

Lucas revised his estimate of the American's age. Was it possible that he could be around thirty? Lucas had observed that there was a type of American, looking radiant, over-fit, a smiler, who might be of a newly-discovered species, perhaps from another galaxy, unlike most Americans he had met who were late middle-aged and running to waste. But presumably they had offspring, and perhaps the young man before him was one of these.

'What was that?' Lucas said. 'I was far away.'

'I wondered if you knew Berlin well.'

'I've done very little travel. A bit as a young man, but presidents don't see a lot of the world from the inside of their car. I can't say I miss it. Trespassing around the world is a European habit.'

The American's goat milk arrived.

'So what do you have to say to me?'

The American frowned and looked suddenly older. 'We want you to know that we have not forgotten you.'

'The "we" being who?'

'My brief is to say no more than I have said.'

Lucas thought that at least he had been the subject of a briefing. A comfort of sorts.

'It does not sound a very extensive briefing,' Lucas said.

'I'm just passing on a message, sir.'

'That's it?'

'Yup.'

'Nothing more?'

'My brief.'

'No need to apologise. I am good at riddles.'

'Let me say this: we had a little meeting at the embassy. We wanted to make contact with you again. How should we do it without compromising you, and ourselves? Let's keep it informal, I said, let the doctor know how we feel, on a one to one basis. No need to have a minder to take notes.'

'You can always deny it.'

'We trust you, doctor.'

'Is that wise?'

The American smiled, but still looked older. 'We know you can be a hard man, but we believe that you know where your interests are.'

'And where are they?'

'I have already said too much.'

The American signalled for the bill, examined it and placed it on the table with a neat pile of coins.

'Do you have six-p, doctor?'

Lucas added a small silver coin to the pile. He got up. 'Thanks for the hospitality. I hope to return it.' He held out his hand. 'Can I ask how old you are?'

'Why is that?'

'I collect ages.'

'I am in my thirty-seventh year.'

Lucas left the Ritz by the Piccadilly door and turned left and entered Green Park. He could walk through the park to his flat.

There were two nearly adjoining parks in what Lucas had come to regard as his domain. The other was St James's Park. Both were once part of the royal hunting grounds that provided a means for the king to kill something other than time. Of the two, Green Park, although now really no more than a decent sized paddock, had retained a vestige of its old rough ways. The dogs that exercised in St James's Park tended to be kept on leads. Those that exercised in Green Park ran joyously free and shitted on the footpaths.

Lucas watched a young woman who was removing shit from the shoes of the two children in her charge. She seemed to have run out of paper tissues. Lucas liked to talk to people on his walks. At home, when he talked to people, they were flattered; it might be the highlight of their day, their life. Lucas was trying to adjust from being a somebody, the somebody, to being an almost nobody. He accepted that the figure he cut as he paced the footpaths of the park, his head slightly bowed, his hands behind him, was at best a harmless one, and might possibly be regarded as sinister. Most people, he had found, would respond politely, if surprisedly, to a 'Good afternoon' but they would not care to prolong the conversation. He was on 'Good afternoon' terms with a number of people who presumably lived or worked nearby and regularly walked in the park and had become used to seeing him, but so far none had offered any further acquaintance.

'Let me lend you my handkerchief,' Lucas said to the young woman.

The handkerchief was clearly expensive and looked new, straight from the box, not even laundered. It was a shock to be offered this when you were cleaning shit from a child's shoe. The shock of the new? It was difficult to say. Perhaps if the young women was interested in art, the thought might have come to her that this was the sort of surrealistic gesture that Marcel Duchamp might have made when he was walking in the Luxembourg Gardens, between inventing ready-mades. It would show that no knowledge is wasted, even if it only enables you to make unusual thought associations while cleaning shit from shoes. Lucas, it should be said, did not look like an artist intent on demonstrating the shock of the new. He was certainly not French. He did not fit immediately into the simple categories of men that the young woman encountered in the park: those who tried to pick her up by offering chat about the children, or the seemingly harmless ones who have children of their own. This man had no children in sight, but nor did he seem to be flirtatious. He was merely offering a handkerchief.

The woman shook her head vigorously, to the point of impoliteness. She was in that state known to mothers and suffragan mothers of being on the brink of losing control. She had one child on her lap, trying to keep its shoes from soiling her topcoat, and not far away was the other child circling another pile of dog shit. The offer of the handkerchief seemed merely stupid. She felt a hatred for the inhabitants of the detached world, especially Duchamp, had she thought of him. But then she found a reserve supply of tissues. She uttered a dreadful warning to the child near the shit, and this deterred it from tormenting her further. Normality was saved.,

'I am sorry to have been so abrupt,' she said. 'It was extremely kind of you.'

Lucas put away his handkerchief. 'You will want to see a doctor?', adding, when the woman looked puzzled, 'For the germs?'

'I don't think so.'

'English dogs do not have germs?'

'Of course they do. Filthy tykes.'

'Tykes?'

'Dogs. Tykes, filthy ones.'

'Excuse me. Of course.'

'You are a doctor?'

'Not a medical doctor.'

'I see.' Uncertainty. 'You are on holiday, business?'

'I live here. Very near here.' Lucas pointed in the general direction of a row of houses overlooking the park. 'There. The white house with the black door.'

'All of it?'

'I have an apartment. Would you like to see it?'

When the women did not answer immediately he said, 'My wife would be charmed to offer you some tea. She loves meeting English people.'

The girl had had a wearisome afternoon, she was slightly bored and it was still only half past three. There was something interesting, even pleasantly ugly, about a man who apparently did not mind his home being invaded by two grubby children and their keeper.

'I'd love a cup of tea.'

The encounter had been noticed by Helen Berlin. She had not been following Lucas, far from it. She was on her rounds. The royal parks' police are immensely knowledgeable about the lives of the people who were rich and well connected enough to live in this favoured neighbourhood. Lucas, they had observed, was a decent gentleman who made a habit of nodding to passers-by.

What routine did you follow, Officer, in your duties as minder? Well, nothing much. It was terribly boring, to be honest. I did not want to alarm Mr Lucas by constantly knocking on his door, but I kept up general surveillance. *Meaning what?* Well, I spoke to the park police whose patrols took them regularly past the house where Mr Lucas was living. *Thank you, Miss Berlin, that will be all for the moment.* Cover your back. Very vulnerable, backs.

Helen had in fact been speaking to a park policeman when Lucas and his new friend came into view.

'Inspector!'

Helen briefly wondered if Lucas had spotted someone else, but it was clear that she was his quarry.

'Mr President!' she said. One title deserved another.

'This is very fortunate,' Lucas said. He grasped Helen's hand warmly. 'We are just about to have a cup of English tea. Please join us.'

Helen sought a suitable excuse. She was working on a case. She was on her way to see her lover. She had something in her eye that needed urgent medical attention. She looked at the girl and her two charges that Lucas had found under a stone in the park. What was the girl doing accepting hospitality from a stranger? Jenkins said no more visits to Lucas. But did that now apply with his latest instruction to wrap things up? Helen made the gesture of looking at her wristwatch. 'Just a quick one then?'

Lucas's wife was out.

'Perhaps she had some English people to meet?' Helen said.

'Perhaps,' Lucas said, uncertainly, not sure whether Helen was making a joke. 'Never mind, we shall still have tea. And something nice for the small ones.'

The small ones' shoes had been left at the door, and the small ones themselves were standing, hand in hand, in the middle of the huge living room, looking at the ceiling on which was painted a tableau of women in what looked like thin dresses.

'They are good, your children,' he said to the girl from the park.

'Probably plotting something.'
'You speak like a fond mother.'
'Their mother is dead.'
'Ah. Then you are a friend?'
'Their nanny.'
'The English nanny?'
'That's it.'
'They are very famous, the English nannies?'
'I suppose so. Like Huntley and Palmer's biscuits.'
'I had an English nanny once. Not wholly English, but she had lived in England. You follow?'

The conversation about nannies was concluded by the arrival of tea, on a large trolley trundled in by an elderly Asian woman, as it had been on Helen's previous visit. Helen had the subversive thought that perhaps it was the same pile of carbohydrates in many forms that had been offered to her, preserved in some traditional Asian way. As before, Helen and Lucas ate frugally. 'The little ones will help us out,' Lucas predicted.

The little ones had each taken a plate but, seemingly awed by the display of food before them, were looking to their nanny for guidance. She cut each of them a piece of current bread and spread the slices with strawberry jam. She took a muffin for herself. A quarter of an hour later she and the two children were still eating.

'I think you've had enough. Your tummies will be bursting.'
'But we are still hungry, Nanny Cathy.'
'Just one more cake, then. We don't want the kind man to think we are greedy.'

Helen, Lucas and Nanny Cathy watched several more cakes being conveyed into tummies, where presumably they were being separated into their original elements.

But children tire eventually even of eating. The two had now got on to the floor, playing some game; trains perhaps, Helen thought. Did children still play trains? Lucas, she noted, was watching them anxiously. Whatever experiences Lucas had had as a dictator, presumably minding children was not among them. He was probably now regretting his encounter in the park.

'No, no, no, no, no.' This was a cry from the nanny. She swooped on one of the children, put her fingers into its mouth and withdrew what looked like a small metal ball. Lucas moved to take it, but Helen was nearer. One moment it was in her hand, the next it was in her pocket. 'Must have been a button I dropped,' she said. 'Sorry about that. Is he all right?'

Lucas was scrutinising Helen's clothes.

'May I see the button?' he said.

Helen went through the motions of searching her pockets.

'Must have fallen into one of the hems,' she said. 'Time to do some stitching.' She offered Lucas a smile. He did not smile back. Helen was aware that her pulse rate had increased, but not, she thought, worryingly. In the police pulse rates are routinely raised. The simplest police duty, just talking to a motorist who has misbehaved, can send it briefly aflutter. Within moments Helen felt her rate resume its normal unnoticed rhythm. She waited while Lucas considered his options, and assumed, and hoped, that they did not include violence. But whatever they were became irrelevant. The child who had created the crisis in the living room was now being sick. It was an unusually comprehensive vomit. The child had obviously eaten well that day. Breakfast and lunch surfaced, along with a generous helping from the tea trolley.

'I'm terribly, terribly sorry, doctor,' said the nanny. 'I'll clean it all up.'

'I am sure you would, my dear. But a maid will do that. I think you should get the little one into the fresh air, and I am sure he will soon feel better.'

'Is that all right, sir?'

'Quite all right, Nanny Cathy.'

'It was a lovely tea. Sorry it was all spoiled.'

'There will be other teas, I'm sure.'

But not, Helen thought, for nannies and their children in this apartment.

'We'll be on our way, then.'

'I think you should.' A slight tone of impatience had moved into Lucas's voice.

'I'll come with you a little way,' Helen said. 'You'd better get a taxi.'

Lucas shrugged his shoulders. Had he accepted defeat? 'I hope I may see you again, inspector. At my party, perhaps?'

Helen thought not. The way things were moving Lucas would have his party in jail.

'I hope so, Mr President.' Weasel words, but they had their uses.

As Helen, the nanny and the two children walked away from Green Park, the nanny said, 'I didn't think it was a button. It was more a sharp metal thing.'

Helen fingered the spent bullet in her pocket.

'Careless, anyway, for it to be left lying around.'

THIRTEEN

Helen believed that she had enough information for Lucas to be arrested. A rubber bag containing the body of a male, aged about 25, had been recovered from the Thames. He had apparently died from a bullet in his head. A passport identified the man as a native of Sulu. He had apparently arrived at Heathrow on a short-term visa. A lot of apparentlys. The details were circulated to all police forces, but initially did not produce a response. If Sulu was known at all, it was distinguished by its political instability, but it happened that someone at the Yard with a knowledge of geography remembered that its president had sought sanctuary in Britain. Anyone know anything about him? There's a girl called Berlin who is supposed to be nurse-maiding him. Better send her the stuff about the corpse in the Thames. Might be a link.

Helen had noticed on her second visit to Lucas that the east side of Green Park, where his flat was located, was watched over by surveillance cameras. She checked whether they were working, in her experience not always a feature of surveillance systems. Surprisingly, they were. The Queen took an interest in the circuits installed in the parks around her palace to protect her and had appointed a Lord Chamberlain of Electronics, or some such, to check that they were maintained in good order and dusted regularly. Helen spent several hours running through recordings made on the day the Sulu man had arrived in Heathrow. They were of a tedium that only a fan of the music of John Cage would enjoy, but eventually Helen's endurance was rewarded. A tape showed a man of Asian appearance arriving at the building where Lucas had his flat. Fifteen minutes later another man in overalls came out of the building with a bundle over his shoulder. The bundle went into the boot of his car, and he drove away quickly. Helen compared the time of these events with the arrival time of the aircraft bringing the Sulu man to London. The times corresponded roughly, assuming that the Sulu man had come to Lucas's flat straight from the airport. Helen rewound the tape a little and found the man in overalls arriving in his car. Helen noted the registration number, which could be checked. The bullet she had picked up from the floor of Lucas's sitting room matched the bullet taken from the Sulu corpse. Forensics said it had been fired from the same gun.

Helen was writing a report of her findings. She was at home, or what she called her home; one room, what at one time would have been called a bed-sitting-room with 'facilities', a tiny bathroom and a tinier kitchen, but which was now described by estate agents without noticeable embarrassment as a studio. The rent took half of Helen's salary. It was, said Helen's parents, a preposterous amount to pay. Her father said he knew of whole houses where the rent was less. But her parents lived in several acres in Kent, far from the central London district where Helen managed with an expensive few square feet.

To the casual eye the place looked in disorder, but Helen was comfortable with what she called her system. Her desktop contained only a small computer and a printer. On the floor and on the bed were perhaps a dozen pieces of paper with notes on them. From time to time Helen would leave her desk, select a note, return to the desk and resume her report. Just the facts; it would be for others to make deductions, if any. Either a murder was committed during the fifteen minutes of recording that Helen had isolated; or nothing special had happened. There were other flats in the building. The man in overalls could have been picking up some innocent package rather than a corpse. The Asian man in the recording might now be happily eating a plate of curry.

Anyone could pick holes in Helen's theory that a murder has taken place in the flat, probably by Lucas, and there were plenty at the Yard who would be happy to do so. Circumstantial evidence, and not much of that, eh, Miss Berlin? The request the Yard had made to her about a possible link between the Thames corpse and Lucas had been a formality, and her investigation had probably been more thorough than was required. In the war against crime it was a tiny incident hardly worth mentioning in the day's communiqués. In some ways the war against crime was more relentless that conventional war, which had lulls and breakthroughs and an eventual end. Crime never surrendered. It became stronger and cleverer. In the war to which Helen had committed herself, the policy was of containment of the enemy; elimination was not even considered. The possible murder of a foreigner and the dumping of his body was of course a serious matter, to be investigated as far as resources allowed. It was not an apparent threat to containment. Like a thousand other crimes, major or minor, reported each day, it was likely to be left unsolved, although not closed.

But should Lucas at least be questioned? Helen sensed he might kill again. That was not evidence, circumstantial or otherwise. But what was the point of being a copper if you could not sense menace? Helen clicked the save button on her computer, printed the report and put it in an envelope. It was now a little after midnight and chilly. Helen put on a topcoat, walked to the Yard, left the report with a messenger, walked home and went to bed. The report could have been left until the morning. Jenkins might not read it even then. But it belonged to the Yard, and you didn't keep the Yard waiting. That was the rule .

Helen awoke feeling the need to talk to someone, preferably someone prepared to do the duty of a wall against which she could bounce her thoughts. Not Robinson, now a lackey of Lucas.

Joel Butcher would be prepared to do wall duty, but in return Helen would have to listen to yet another argument about why she should go on television. She called Carruthers Smith.

FOURTEEN

The desk that Helen had used on her first day at the Foreign Office had now been re-occupied by the man who had been to Uzbekistan and lived in Coulsdon. 'Ah. The sleuth in stockings,' he said. Not much of a joke, Helen thought, but what could you expect from a man who used ribbed condoms? However, Smith seemed welcoming and appeared genuinely keen to know how she had been getting on.

'Where have you been? We thought you had deserted us.'

'Oh, you know, checking people's television licences, being officious, the important things that police do.'

'And seeing Lucas?'

Helen said nothing. What was Lucas up to now?

'Don't look so stern, Miss Berlin. Lucas called me, said how practical you were, and sensitive. Practical and sensitive, they were his words. We are grateful. A tricky customer. Did you get my note?'

'It's probably in a pigeonhole at the Yard.'

'I copied it to your boss. I know how these things work.'

'Well, thanks.'

'Now, a celebration cup of coffee?'

Smith disappeared to where coffee was made in the Foreign Office. Helen considered the small but not unpleasant development that had occurred in the past minute or two. It came to her that she was now free to draw a line under the Lucas business and return to whatever duties lay ahead at the Yard, student sergeant, mission accomplished, client satisfied, even self-satisfied. Smith had provided a brownie point that would do her no harm. Quit while you are on top. It was a temptation. Wrap it up, Jenkins had said. This could be the wrap. Her report was now presumably in the depths of someone's pending tray. But should a copper walk away from a possible murder? But she wasn't walking away. She was part of a team. She had done quite well, she told herself, for a constable not quite a sergeant. She had, what?, risked her life, kept her cool and put together a possible case.

When Smith returned Helen said, 'There are a few things you should know about Lucas.'

Smith proved to be an attentive listener, interrupting rarely and only to ask thoughtful questions. Perhaps she had underrated him. Later, when she came to recall what she had said during the hour or so they had spent together, she wondered if she should have been more guarded, not straying from the facts in her report to the Yard; not offering Smith her own views. But then, she had gone to see Smith primarily to explore her own random thinking. At the end of her near monologue Smith said that it was useful that she had been so frank; more than useful, important. 'I want to say this, Miss Berlin. You have acted entirely correctly. Let me be clear. I shudder to think what would have happened if you'd had Lucas arrested. Very sensitive.'

'He might yet. The handcuffs are ready.'

Smith gave what seemed to Helen to be a real shudder. 'Deeply political. Not forgetting the diplomatic aspect. America, all that. Very sensitive.'

'Someone else's worry. I'm winding down.'

'Leaving us?' Smith seemed almost moved.

'We can always be friends.'

But Smith wasn't smiling.

Impulsively, Helen leaned forward and pecked Smith on the cheek. 'There. Kissed by a copper. Doesn't happen often. Thanks for the coffee.'

Half a minute after leaving Helen put her head around the door. 'I probably don't need to say this, but be discreet. What I've told you is still confidential. I don't want to get a reputation as a blabbermouth.'

'This is entirely confidential,' Smith said later on the phone to his contact at the American Embassy. 'Can we switch to secure?'

'Should we do lunch?'

'Good idea.'

FIFTEEN

They met at Bentleys in Swallow Street, which is about midway between the American Embassy and the Foreign Office, and where the diners are seated in alcoves, which at least give the impression of privacy.

At the end of the oysters course the American said, 'Do you believe her?'

'Helen Berlin is trustworthy,' Smith said. 'And sensible.'

'Pretty?'

'I'd say so.'

'Sexy?'

'I dare say.'

'I like a uniform.'

'Detectives wear civilian clothes.'

When the Dover sole arrived, the American said, 'The new lot in Sulu are out to get Lucas. They hate him.'

'You sound very sure.'

'No doubt about it. Top gen.'

Smith waited for the American to elaborate. Top gen sounded a dated phrase, but had, who knows, perhaps been reborn in the intelligence world. You never could tell with language. But the American did not elaborate. He repeated, 'Top gen.'

'The chap in the Thames was sent to kill Lucas?'

'Of course,' said the American.

Of course? Smith felt a touch irritated with his lunch companion. There were pointers to a murder, no more. Helen had been keen to emphasise that. Strong pointers, but no 'of course'.

The American seemed to sense that he had hijacked Smith's story, for he said, 'I agree there's no presumption.'

'But you think Lucas killed him instead?'

'That would follow,' said the American, now retreating into the conditional.

'They will try again?'

'That too would follow.'

'And succeed?'

'Who knows? King Zog survived fifty-five assassination attempts and died naturally in his own bed.'

Smith was vaguely aware of the name but would not wish to be pressed to put a country to it. Somewhere in the Balkans probably. One of the hazards of being in the Foreign Office was that people assumed you were familiar with every nook and cranny in the world. It could be tricky at receptions. 'Ah, Smithy, the very man.' And you would be stuck for the next fifteen minutes with the culture minister of Tum-Tum Land. Smith was reckoned to be an expert on the former Soviet countries of Central Asia, but the places he knew really well were Italy and France, where he took his family for holidays.

As Smith made a miniature sandwich of two water-biscuits and a scraping of goat's cheese, he said, 'Lucas is expendable, I suppose. Nasty for us if he is killed, but we will have done our best, and the world will still go on turning.'

'But perhaps not turning quite so reliably.'

Smith divided the remains of a bottle of Chablis with his companion, and was tempted to order a glass of red to go with the coffee. On the other hand, it might make him drowsy for the afternoon. He was still stuck with the Brazil business the Yard had dumped on him. Now what was the American on about? The world not turning?

'What do you know about Sulu?' the American said.

Here we go again. 'Central Asia is my patch.'

The American took the answer to be 'nothing'. He said, 'There are only two things you need to know about Sulu. One is that it has the best harbour in Asia. The other is that the harbour is American.'

'On lease from the government, I take it?'

'In theory, yes. In reality, a bit of America, the bit that keeps the peace in Asia. If the Chinese threaten to invade Taiwan, a carrier from Sulu will move to the Taiwan Strait to hint that this would not be a good idea. That sort of thing. Speak softly and carry a big stick, as Reagan said.'

Smith was sure that Teddy Roosevelt said it, but perhaps Reagan said it too. A memory suddenly came to Smith of a newspaper picture of Ronald Reagan and Lucas together. God, that was a long time ago. How long? It must have been when Reagan was president and he was on a goodwill visit to Sulu to show American solidarity. Sulu: of course he remembered it. Things were falling into place now. That was the thing about the Foreign Office. You had to know a bit about everything.

'I can't understand why you kicked Lucas out,' Smith said.

'Kicked out?' The American examined the words. 'It was his own people that kicked him out, his cronies, the military, the church, even the ordinary people. All we did was to get him out before he was lynched.'

'You'd have him back?'

'We have to work with the people. Even in a dump like Sulu there is public opinion. Lucas was our man. But he got too greedy.'

'And the new strong man: not so greedy?'

'A woman. We don't know whether she is strong or not. We don't know whether she is greedy. We are more worried that she is a nationalist, that is, anti-American.'

'Yanks go home?'

'That was her campaign message.'

'Awkward.'

'If she means it.'

'You'd lose your little bit of America?'

'Or she would lose her job.'

'And Lucas would be back?'

'That sounds too simple. The mob that threw him out might change its mind, but not without some pressure; a bit of hardship if American aid suddenly dried up. A touch of poverty, particularly of the grinding sort. But these things take time to work. We do need to keep Lucas alive, if only as a threat to the stupid bitch to toe the line.'

'Superpower politics?'

'We are an apprentice superpower. We have little experience of world control. We are not Rome of the Caesars, with hundreds of years of experience of bringing opponents to heel. Our Caesar is a hick from the mid-west. He talks of regime change, but look what is happening in Afghanistan. The Taliban are winning. The farmers are planting opium and economy is thriving on heroin. Justice means cutting off people's hands. Women are still covered from head to foot, not wearing high heels and lipstick.'

'I thought I might round off with a red wine.'

'I'll join you.'

Smith ordered a bottle, and it was mid-afternoon before lunch was declared over. The American insisted on paying with his debit card, a black one, Smith noted, but had refused Smith's offer to share.

'My treat next time?'

'Sure.'

Back at his office, Smith did not feel like working. Still, he should make some notes about the lunch. Making a note after a meeting was holy work in the Foreign Office, a record to be filed away for thirty years so that after you were dead your successor could find out what really happened. Smith wrote the name Lucas on a notepad. He had to be kept alive in case the Americans needed him back in Sulu. That might arise if the new woman there did not suit the Americans. That was clear enough. She might try to throw out the Americans from their vital harbour. Clear, too, but Smith wished he had asked more about the harbour: how important was it? There were harbours everywhere. But he had not wanted to look like a questioning idiot. The American had anyway been unnecessarily superior with his 'of course' about Helen's murder theory.

Smith picked up his phone and dialled an internal number.

'Gladys?'

'That sounds like a good lunch.'

'A little respect please, Gladys.'

'What can I do for you, Smithy?'

Smith had known Gladys since she had started in the research department twelve years ago.

'Sulu?'

'A country.'

'Much on it?'

'Large amounts.'

'The American harbour there?'

'A base really. Lots on that too.'

When Smith paused Gladys said, 'What about a postcard?'

A postcard was the essentials; sometimes less than that. Postcards saved diplomats in emergencies.

'Perfect..'

'I'll send it down, Smithy. Postcard and black coffee.'

Sulu, the postcard said, had America's largest overseas military base. The harbour could take the biggest carriers; the airfield the biggest transports. So that explained why Sulu was important to the apprentice superpower. But what especially impressed Smith was that the Americans had made themselves so comfortable. The place had tennis courts, swimming pools, a golf course. No wonder they hated the idea of leaving. The postcard said the place was self-sufficient, with its own power and water, but it probably could not survive an eviction notice from the Sulu government. The British had hoped to hold on to Hong Kong, but in the end they had to go.

As Smith was preparing to leave for home, he had a call from the American at the embassy.

'The ambassador is concerned.'

'I'm not surprised.'

'How are you fixed for a breakfast meeting?'

A breakfast meeting was a euphemism for an early call and a stale croissant.

'I could manage about nine, perhaps a quarter to.'

'We are thinking of seven.'

Smith's wife would have to do the school run.

'If you must.'

'Good man.'

Good man. Top gen. Archaic English spoken with a New York accent.

Smith was about to ask who else would be at the meeting, but the American had hung up. Smith called Helen Berlin's number. She should be told what he had done with her 'entirely confidential' information. There was no reply and he left a message to call him. However, next morning in Grosvenor Square as he was walking towards the American Embassy, he heard his name called. He turned. Helen was hurrying toward him.

'I tried to call you at home,' she said. 'Is your phone always engaged?'

Probably, Smith thought, with one or other of his daughters. 'Perhaps a fault on the line,' he said. He looked at his watch. Ten minutes to the meeting. Was there time to brief Helen, and to listen to her indignation? Perhaps not.

'It looks like someone at the Yard read my report,' she said. 'But I suppose odder things have happened.'

Ah. Smith sensed a reprieve. Perhaps this was going to be a good day.

'But are they going to charge Lucas with murder?' Helen said. 'Is that what this meeting is about?'

'I think the idea is to look at the big picture,' Smith said cautiously.

'You know something,' Helen said. 'Come on Carruthers Smith. Out with it.'

Smith tapped his watch. 'We'll be late. All will emerge, Helen. Be patient.'

The ambassador thanked everyone for turning out at what he called 'this godforsaken hour', even if it was to put the world right. Smith warmed to him. He looked the part, reassuring, polite, in charge, even though he was a billionaire who had been given London after contributing extravagantly to the American president's election campaign

'I think we all know each other,' the ambassador said. However, this assumption did not seem to be shared by several of the company, whose response was to look to their neighbours, as though to confirm that they had never set eyes on them before. Smith knew the American who had paid for their boozy lunch the previous day. He supposed he now knew the American ambassador, whose hand he had shaken when he arrived. He knew Helen. He did not know the middle-aged man in a police uniform who was sitting next to Helen, but assumed he was Helen's boss Jenkins. He did not know the man sitting next to the ambassador, but his uniform and badges disclosed that he was in the United States army, was a two-star general and that his name was Ripley. He did not know the woman with a big notebook and a pencil poised, but presumed that she was the ambassador's secretary. Seven people, including Smith. The table they were sitting at was laid for nine, albeit in rudimentary way, plate, knife and cup and saucer. A simple breakfast.

The ambassador was describing the American base at Sulu, providing what seemed to Smith to be an extraordinary amount of technical detail about its military efficiency, but not mentioning the comfort provided for its inhabitants that had so impressed Smith. Perhaps the ambassador, being a billionaire, assumed that luxury was normal for Americans. He said Sulu had been liberated by the United States from Spain in the early 20th century, and introduced to democracy. Lucas, he said, had in recent times disappointed the Americans, but America was not ungrateful for the support he had given to the free world in the past. Sulu under Lucas had supported America in the Vietnam War. He himself had enjoyed the best of hospitality from Lucas during two visits to Sulu on business trips during the Reagan presidency. 'We are glad that our English friends are able to provide him with a safe haven while we see what transpires in Sulu under the new regime there.'

The ambassador smiled in Smith's direction. Smith was cooling towards the ambassador and did not return the smile. A revisionist view of Lucas was being offered by the ambassador. Not a tyrant, but an old friend. The Foreign Office was used to revisionism, and was itself a practised hand at the craft, but it shouldn't be forced. Yes, that was the word, forced. Smith helped himself to a stale croissant, his second. A hovering attendant refilled his cup with coffee. Good coffee. The Americans were good with coffee. 'However,' the ambassador continued, 'I have to say that we are concerned for Lucas's safety. We know one attempt has been made on his life. The new regime, we fear, is composed of ruthless people, and its reach extends even into London. I think General Ripley would like to say something at this point.'

'Let me ask the key question,' the general said. 'What protection is President Lucas getting?'

The ambassador turned to the man sitting next to Helen. 'Superintendent?'

'The very best that Scotland Yard can provide,' he said.

'So if I said to you,' the general said, 'can you tell me what at this precise moment are the president's movements, could you tell me? You get my drift, a twenty-four hour watch?'

'I'd say he was probably having his breakfast, as we are. Eh, Helen?'

'Almost certainly he still in bed. The accident knocked him up a bit.'

Six pairs of eyes focused on Helen Berlin. It was, Smith thought later, a rare and choice moment, made all the more so by Helen's matter of fact manner.

'Nothing serious,' Helen said. 'But it shook him up a bit.'

'An accident?' the general said. 'Are you telling me that President Lucas has had an accident?'

...

It was raining when Lucas set out on the journey that was to end with an accident. A fuzzy drizzle was falling in Green Park, but plenty of light seemed to be coming through Lucas's vast, though unobtrusive, windows. The houses in St James's had the first call on whatever light was available. Lucas opened a window. The fine rain had turned to heavy rain and he could hear it falling evenly on the trees in the park. Lucas thought of a woman turning herself this way and that under a shower. He thought he would like to see a Rubens or a Degas. Lucas's libido had quiet tastes.

He put on a coat and hat. Outside, he exchanged greetings with the park policeman that, since Helen's visit, he regarded as his, and turned towards Pall Mall and the National Gallery in Trafalgar Square. London, Lucas had decided, was a generous city. You might live in a garret but the resources of a great house were at your disposal without charge: the parks, the incomparable collections of pictures. He ascribed this generosity to the Queen. He had met her; not perhaps in quite the familiar way he suggested in his letter, but they did speak at a reception.

She said, 'I should very much like to visit your country one day, Mr President.' He could not recall what reply he made, but no doubt it was courteous. He was cheered she lived nearby and wondered if by chance he might encounter her. In his occasional walks around the district he had noted a number of royal crests in shop windows and assumed that the Queen did most of her shopping locally, accompanied no doubt by a lady companion who would fill the royal basket with wine, tobacco, chocolates and rich foods that the Queen's subjects had been warned off for fear of heart attacks.

In the National Gallery Lucas found his eyes were drifting from its bewitching images to the brass plates on the frames that recorded the life spans of the artists. For some reason a succession of artists whose ages he calculated had all died at sixty-five. Lucas was sixty-one. There was no reason why he should have only four years left, but no reason either that he should live longer, or even that he should survive as long. The sixties was not an age when people raised their eyebrows and said, 'Fancy, that was no age.' Perhaps because of this unwelcome encounter with memento mori, Lucas had an adventurous impulse to venture beyond the boundaries of the sanctuary of St James's. He strolled towards Piccadilly. At Fortnum and Mason, one of the outposts of what he had come to regard as his parish, he crossed the street to the Royal Academy of Arts. A banner proclaimed an exhibition of fifty years of British art. It was, Lucas thought, tempting to be able to absorb fifty years of anything in no time at all. The exhibition, though, did not start until the following day. Lucas did a circuit of the academy's quadrangle and noted with approval that the statue of Reynolds had been ennobled with a garland of fresh flowers. It was a felicitous idea that he thought he would carry home with him from exile. If his statue in Sulu has been pulled down, not an impossibility knowing the pettiness of the new regime, he would have a new one elected. He would appoint a nun, or a person of equal probity, to change the flowers each day, for ever; not commonplace tropical flowers, but exotic ones like daffodils imported from a temperate country.

The improbability of Burlington Arcade drew Lucas in. Around him were tourists, confident that they looked rich enough to be fleeced. He turned right at the top of the arcade and found himself in Regent Street. Lucas now felt far from St James's. He could wave his arms for a taxi, which would return him to the haven of the parks. But he was experiencing a remembered pleasure: of venturing from his palace to touch the common people. Should he have filled his pockets with money which he would hand out at random to unsuspected people in the crowd and see their faces glow with surprise? Perhaps not. Judging from the bits of language that had come to Lucas's ears, few of the people in Regent Street were natives. They would be puzzled by his gesture.

He arrived at the clamour of Oxford Circus. This perhaps was far enough. Lucas saw a taxi and stepped into the road. He heard a car's squeal of brakes, and a door slam. He felt a blow to his chest.

'You want to be killed?'

Lucas was on the ground. An angry motorist stood over him. Lucas thought he might have a gun or, worse, a knife: a gun is fantasy but a knife is real. He rolled on his back and drew his legs to his chest. He believed he was going to be kicked. At least his spine and his genitals would be spared. But no blow came, no blade flashed. He was being helped to his feet. Several people were surrounding him. The human being is supposed to be a protected species. The motorist had returned to his car, but someone was hammering on the windscreen and shouted as the car drove away.

'Are you all right now?' A young woman was trying to dust him down.

'You are very kind. Yes, I am perfectly all right.'

'I've got his number. No bloody police around when you want them, of course.' This from the man who had been hammering on the windscreen. He handed Lucas a piece of paper. On it were a car registration number and a name and address and a telephone number. 'I'll be your witness if you want me. Bloody thug.'

'You've all been very kind. It was very unexpected.'

'Too many bloody cars. You a foreigner, too. Don't let it spoil your holiday.'

The crowd of well-wishers dispersed, all except the young woman who was holding on to Lucas's arm. 'Where are you staying? Shall I see you back to your hotel?'

'A taxi would be very useful. That's what I was trying to get.'

The woman signalled a taxi. She seemed to have a way with them. The thought crossed Lucas's mind that he should take her home. She might be useful. But he had taken enough risks for today. He thanked her and said goodbye.

In the taxi Lucas examined his injuries. He had bruises, but was otherwise unhurt. How innocent he was, living his life in an eggshell. That morning he had read in a newspaper that motorists in California, driven to the edge of lunacy by traffic jams, had opened fire on each other. He had not been shot at but he thought, given time, murder would arrive on the roads of England. Motoring was one of the few activities that were both dangerous and boring.

At his flat Lucas went to bed. Helen arrived soon after. The policeman on duty outside the building had called her. 'Looked a bit bruised, Miss, said he was all right, but I thought you'd better know.'

David Robinson answered the door. Beyond him stood the woman who made enormous teas. Helen asked her where her master was. She looked blank.

'I think she speaks French,' Robinson said.

'*Il dors?*' Helen said.

The woman shook her head and pointed to a half open door.

Helen entered. Lucas was indeed awake. He looked still and pale. Helen thought of a corpse laid out for inspection by relations, except that an undertaker would presumably put some colour on the corpse's face.

'What's all this?' Helen touched Lucas's hand.

'I am finished, Miss Berlin. Done for. You'd better go.'

Helen felt his pulse, examined his eyes, pulled back the bed sheet and observed his bruises, the simple attentions that constitute much of medical practice. He did not look done for.

'What happened?'

'My demon has abandoned me.'

The tea woman was at the bedroom door.

'Where is Madam Lucas?' Helen said.

A shrug of the shoulders.

'*Vous comprenez?*'

Another shrug.

Robinson appeared at the door. Helen said, 'Is there anyone in the flat except this dopey woman?'

'No one I've seen. I only arrived a couple of minutes before you. Delivering something for Lucas.' Robinson held up an envelope, as though to confirm the innocence of his mission.

Helen left the flat, had a brief talk to the policeman outside about what the taxi driver had said and returned to Lucas's room. She sat on the bed and took his hand. 'I don't think you are seriously damaged, Mr Lucas, but you have had a shock. You fell over?'

'My demon..'

'We all have demons. Nasty things. You went out. Where to?'

Lucas had closed his eyes. 'You are kind. The English are a kind people.'

'The taxi driver told the policeman he picked you up at Oxford Circus. Do you remember that?'

At the end of perhaps fifteen minutes of coaxing Helen felt that she had a reasonably true account of Lucas's adventure. She decided it had not been another attempt on his life. He had simply been stupid.

Helen returned to the living room with its heavy doors that she had banged on when she was kept prisoner. Curiosity told her to open one. It led to a room quite as big as the living room. Another door opened to a wide corridor lined with books. She wondered what she was looking for. Perhaps an Asian slave. Perhaps nothing.

Robinson was sitting in the living room looking at the Sulu book. Helen said, 'David, I'm going out now. I'll arrange for a doctor to see Lucas, and a nurse to keep the rascal company. Hang around here until they arrive. Okay?'

'All right. But Helen, can we talk?'

'Who can tell?' And then she was gone.

...

'When exactly did this happen?' the American ambassador asked when Helen gave a brief account of the accident at the embassy meeting.

'Yesterday afternoon.'

'And he has recovered?'

'Yes.'

'Out of bed?'

'Yes.'

'You have done well, Constable.'

'Thank you, sir.'

The ambassador paused to allow the meeting to endorse his approval of Helen's actions. There was indeed a quiet murmuring, which Helen took to mean at least a majority verdict in her favour. The general, she assumed, would dissent. He had not been pleased at being taken by surprise.

'Constable Berlin has undoubtedly done her best in a difficult situation,' the general said. Ah, thought Helen, subtle stuff, an attack on the flank. 'I too commend her sensible conduct. What concerns me is that the protection of President Lucas has been left to one young woman and, apparently, a London bobby whose duties are normally to stop people walking on the grass. What I propose is that the president be moved to a safe place with an armed guard. I will be happy to arrange this, and it can be done quickly, today if necessary.'

Not bad, Helen thought. A soldier's solution. Put the problem under guard and forget it. But stupid. Lucas would not stand being made a virtual prisoner. He would hire expensive lawyers who would make all kinds of fuss. He would probably write to the Queen again.

Jenkins said that it was an excellent idea. A predictable response, Helen thought. Dump the problem on someone else.

Carruthers Smith said he believed that the Foreign Office had provided excellent protection for Lucas under the professional guidance of Miss Berlin. However, he accepted that Lucas, if he were a problem, was an American problem. That being so, he would have no objection to the general's plan. The Foreign Office would obviously like to be kept informed of Lucas's whereabouts. Would the safe place be in the embassy, which had the diplomatic status of American territory, or elsewhere in Britain?

'Mr Ambassador,' the general began, but stopped when the ambassador raised a restraining hand.

'Perhaps,' the ambassador said, 'I could clarify a couple of points. First, this is not just an American problem. We share the problem with Britain, which has generously provided Lucas with sanctuary. Second, although the general has politely referred to President Lucas, he is not now a president. I do not want to convey the idea that the United States government regards Lucas as the rightful president of Sulu. Whether he ever will be again is in the realm of fanciful speculation. Certainly we want him to remain in good health. There has been concern about an apparent attempt to kill him, though nothing proved. He has had the accident, which Constable Berlin has dealt with so competently. We have an old saying in Virginia. If a thing ain't broke, don't fix it.'

It was an old saying pretty well everywhere else if you were looking for an excuse for doing nothing, Helen thought.

Two men were standing at the door of the room, apparently waiting to be invited to join the meeting. 'We seem to be late,' one said.

'Very late,' the ambassador said . 'In fact I think we have come to the end of our discussions. Yes, general?'

'My I say with respect, Mr Ambassador, that I wish to put on record that, notwithstanding Constable Berlin's assurances, I am not satisfied that President Lucas is being given suitable protection and I reserve my right to pursue the matter further.'

'Thank you, general. You have made your point with your usual forthrightness. I now close the meeting.'

'What do you think?' said Helen as she and Smith walked away from the embassy.

'Coffee pretty good. Not sure about the croissants. Yesterday's, I think, but warmed up. I supposed they made an effort.'

'Can you talk seriously?'

'Oh dear. Do idiots deserve to be taken seriously?'

'You are a great help, I must say.'

'Do you need help, Miss Berlin? I thought you came out of it well. Helen Berlin the competent. No one says such nice things about me.'

'But what am I suppose to do?'

'Carry on as before. I thought that was the ambassador's message. What does the boss say?'

'He is a bit miffed that the Yard is still lumbered with the Lucas. But for the moment he is probably happy to leave the matter in the charge of the least important member of his team.'

'Well, rest on your laurels. Get on with your studies.'

'What about the general?'

'He had to say something.'

'I'm not so sure,' Helen said. 'He doesn't think Lucas had an accident. He thinks the dreaded Sulu assassins were operating in Oxford Circus.'

'Perhaps they were.'

Helen stopped. Smith stopped. Helen said, 'Whose side are you on, Carruthers Smith?'

'Yours, Miss Berlin, till the world makes sense. And while we are waiting let me show you where we can get a croissant, guaranteed freshly made today.'

'Thanks, but another time.' Jenkins was hovering near. 'Things to do.'

Jenkins was heading towards the Yard. Helen fell in beside him.

'What did you think, sir?'

'Several things, Helen. Several things.'

Jenkins talked even more slowly when he was walking than when he was sitting at his desk. But in the course of the next ten minutes or so he made a number of pronouncements, all of which were of deep interest to Helen. He said he was confident the Yard could now end its responsibility for Lucas. Should never have got involved. American affair, whatever the ambassador said. The general had made that clear. Move him to a safe place with an armed guard. Good riddance. There was the matter of Lucas's behaviour. He had brought the lawless ways of Sulu to Britain. There had been a gunfight in his flat. We did not know the details, but someone had been killed. For the moment though Lucas was immune from prosecution. Jenkins had consulted with his superiors and had been told that the Americans did not want him arrested and that was that. Helen's excellent report had been filed away and would be pursued further should circumstances change. The important thing was that Helen could get on with her career. He thought it possible that she could be made a probationary sergeant, pending the second part of her sergeant's exam. No more money at this stage, of course, in his view she had already earned promotion. Call it decoration in the field.

They had reached the entrance to the Yard, with its strange revolving banner.

Jenkins said, 'Got a bit of leave left?'

'A few days, sir.'

'Better take them now. You're going to be busy from now on.'

SIXTEEN

Helen decided that she would go to Lucas's party for what he called Liberation Day. She liked parties. She was on holiday. She would dress up. She telephoned Lucas. 'Do you mind if I bring a friend?'

Lucas said it was a charming idea. 'May I know your friend's name?'

Helen had first thought of David Robinson as her escort, but had decided he should remain in a state of penance a little longer.

'Joel Butcher. He's a television producer.'

Silence.

'Are you there, Mr Lucas?'

'A pause for thought, Miss Berlin. I have to say that I am not keen on television people. There have been approaches that I have had to disappoint. Part of my conditions of residence, you understand. It would be a discourtesy for me to refuse your friend. But I take it that Mr Butcher would not be my guest in any professional capacity?'

'Naturally not, Mr Lucas. You can take my word for it.'

'I could not ask for anything more reassuring.'

Butcher was enthusiastic about attending Lucas's party, so much so that Helen's suspicions were aroused.

'No television nonsense,' she said. 'Lucas has a thing about it. I've given my word.'

'I'm allowed to watch, I suppose. Or should I be blindfolded?'

'You know what I mean, Joel. And dress respectably. Jacket and tie. No leathers.'

Helen turned her attention to what she should wear.

'What do they wear in Sulu?' Helen asked a friend who had once hitch-hiked to Kathmandu.

'Rags,' she said unhelpfully. 'Lucas robbed them of everything else.'

Helen presumed that Lucas liked women to look simply pretty. Simple prettiness was out of fashion. Helen went to a shop in Covent Garden that was a custodian of the fashions of earlier eras; second-hand clothes but as good as new, far better than new in the opinion of the lady who ran the shop, who called herself Miss Nostalgia.

Helen was attracted to a dress that Miss Nostalgia assured her was worn by a model who sat for Lord Leighton. Helen put it on and added in her imagination the details that would turn her into a pre-Raphaelite divine: her hair a halo of golden curls, her eyes made as big as fruit drops by the application of laudanum. But the dress was expensive, and she did not want to have her hair dyed. She picked instead a dress of the 1950s. It showed her shoulders, its boned bodice drew attention to her breasts and it had a full skirt that emphasised her hips. Miss Nostalgia discovered a pair of shoes with sharp toes and tall heels that both she and Helen agreed might have been made for the dress. As Helen was paying for the clothes, Miss Nostalgia came across a pair of black gloves and a small embroidered evening bag which she insisted on giving her.

'Everyone will love you,' she said.

'That would be awkward,' Helen said.

When she came to dress for the party she found the gloves were too tight. But she put them on anyway.

Joel called for her in a taxi. He was wearing a dinner jacket and black tie, set off with a carnation.

'Past muster?' he said.

'Overdoing it, I'd say.'

Joel said nothing. He gave Helen's 1950s dress a searching look.

'Very well, point taken,' Helen said. 'Girls like to dress up sometimes.'

In the taxi Helen said, 'I thought the party might be off. Lucas had an accident. But he seems to have bounced back. Perhaps his demon has returned.'

'Sorry?'

'Nothing. Just rambling.'

'Anything I should know?'

'Quite likely.'

'A worry shared…'

'I feel out of my depth. You ever get that feeling?'

'All the time.'

Helen took Joel's arm. It was the need for an arm that had prompted her to have a companion for the evening.

'Here we are,' she said. 'Murder mansions.'

'You look really charming, my dear,' Lucas said as she entered the room where the reception for Liberation Day was in progress. Lucas was wearing court dress, black jacket and striped trousers, and on his chest, suspended from a ribbon around his neck, was a decoration, mainly consisting of a large blue stone. He bowed momentarily and kissed Helen's gloved hand, seemingly not noticing the split that had appeared along the forefinger. He gave Joel a double handshake, followed by an arm grip. Perhaps he was relieved that Joel was not heaving a television camera on his shoulder.

'Are you well?' Helen asked politely.

'Extremely well. Quite better.'

'And your wife?'

'Madame Lucas is unfortunately indisposed. She begs you to excuse her. But there are other wives here, and husbands too, who are longing to meet you.' Lucas dismissed his wife's troubles with incongruous joviality. He put an arm around Helen's bare

1950s shoulders and moved her into the room. She found herself talking to an elderly woman who said that she was from Lithuania, that her name was Daugava and asked where Helen came from. Helen hesitated. Did she mean where did she live or where was she born? It did not matter. It was a question Helen never thought it necessary to answer seriously.

'Stepney.'

Daugava repeated the word slowly. It was apparently as foreign to her as Lithuania was to Helen.

'A little farther down the Thames than St James's?'

Helen supposed it was. Daugava made it sound as though the inhabitants strolled along the riverbank in the evening parading their parasols and watching the sun on the river. They did not do that a lot in Stepney.

'It is so nice to see a fresh face. All the others will want to talk to you, but I shall be selfish and keep you to myself for a little while. How did the clever Lucas get to know you?'

'He locked me up.'

This seeming witticism provoked from Daugava a high-pitched laugh, which drew benevolent attention from the rest of the room.

'You have a lovely sense of humour, too. I tell Lucas we need more young people here. We are all so old and we know each other's jokes.'

The guests were indeed not young; some were quite old and one looked very old. He, Daugava said, was the true monarch of the Kingdom of the Two Sicilies. The man he was talking to was from the royal family of Cambodia. Nearby, but not talking, was a priest from North Korea.

Helen's knowledge of geography was being overstretched, but she had grasped a common feature about the people in the room. All were apparently exiles from places where they were once important.

'The main thing,' Daugava said, 'is not to lose heart. These little soirees are important, even though we are getting senile. A party is an assembly of one's most personal possessions. We must keep up our appearances. For some of us it is all we have. Remember how the British always dressed for dinner in savage countries.'

Helen nodded, although uncertain whether in doing do she was agreeing that Britain was a savage country.

'The spirit of St James's is what sustains us,' Daugava said.

'You all live around here?'

'Almost all. If you've got friends and neighbours, as the English say.'

Helen had the bizarre thought of the King of Sicily, the Prince of Cambodia and the Archbishop of Pyongyang leading their fellow exiles in a rousing chorus of the banal song. She looked vaguely around the room. Daugava seemed to assume that Helen was bored with her. 'Now I will tell you something silly about Lucas,' she said invitingly. 'He has been told by an astrologer that he will die in a business suit, so now he tries to wear casual clothes, but he is worried that in London some businessmen wear casual clothes to work.'

'He's wearing formal clothes now.'

'He's being brave, very brave.'

Lucas was passing near to them. Daugava shouted to him, 'Is he coming?' Lucas shrugged. He did not look pleased.

Daugava said. 'I feel so sorry for poor Lucas. The Americans promised to send someone. But not even a valet. It is so humiliating. They will be sorry when that bitch starts makes eyes at the Chinese, if she hasn't already. Then they will be on the telephone quickly enough. "We have a little problem here, Doctor. Be good if you can help us".' Daugava's Lithuanian accent made her imaginary American sound particularly ugly. 'But you must forgive me, my dear. The last thing you want to hear about is our sordid politics.'

'I'm fascinated. Sordid politics sound much more interesting than the ordinary sort.' Another high-pitched laugh from Daugava.

A sentence was forming in Helen's mind, 'I can assure you that the Americans remain very interested in Lucas', but she quickly suppressed it. In return for the brief pleasure of seeing herself suddenly rise in importance, she would be exposing herself to a questionnaire. How do you know? Have you told Lucas? Coppers develop a wariness of falling into such traps, Helen thought. She filed away in her mind the notion that China might be eyeing Sulu. She felt she was beginning to understand something of complexities of Asia.

'I've come to join the fun.' This from the Cambodian prince. He did not look ready for fun. He looked in a sombre mood. Daugava asked him about a house in St John's Wood which has been taken over by squatters who, it seemed, could not be evicted.

'This it seems is the democratic way,' said the prince.

'But it is part of Cambodia,' Daugava said.

'That is the problem,' the prince said, puzzlingly.

'It has to be watched,' Daugava said. 'St John's Wood today, St James's tomorrow, isn't that right, my dear?'

'It is jolly unfair.' Helen spoke with passion. 'You must kick them out.'

The prince and Daugava treated Helen's outburst with a respect that the commonplace remark did not deserve.

'Bravo. The spirit of Dunkirk.'

The prince was not, seemingly, being sarcastic. Perhaps this young woman of spirit would be able to suggest some amazing British way to counter the St John's Wood invasion, and return the building to its rightful owners? Helen suddenly felt she had the attention of other countries with dispossessed representatives who were within earshot. She waited for some helpful thought to come into her mind. She had done the basic course on law that all police go through, but could not remember anything about eviction. It sounded more a civil than a criminal matter. Eventually she said, 'I think you need a fresh mind on the subject. Perhaps you have not consulted the right people.'

'You know of somebody?'

Helen saw Lucas watching her. 'I shall rescue you from these predators,' he said. He took her by the arm and led her to another group where a woman said, 'What a pretty dress.' It was the first time that anyone in the room had specifically mentioned the dress that Helen had taken so much trouble in picking.

'You are kind to say that because…' The sentence was never finished. It was interrupted by the sound of a gun being fired followed by a tinkle of breaking glass. Two men were on the floor, fighting. The man on top was wearing a dinner jacket. A squashed carnation was on the floor nearby. Joel Butcher. The man underneath seemed no longer to be resisting. Lucas was perhaps two yards away. He moved forward, quite slowly, like a footballer measuring his distance, and delivered his right foot into the man's head. Helen heard the thud.

Butcher stood and retrieved his carnation.

'Are you all right, sir?'

'Let's get this creature out of here.'

Lucas took hold of the man's legs and started to drag him towards a door. The King of the Two Sicilies bent down, apparently to help, but stumbled. Someone helped him to his feet. By then Lucas and his burden were through the door. Moments later Lucas reappeared.

'My dear friends, a thousand apologies. Mr Butcher, what can I say? The English, you are heroes.' He clapped his hands in applause. Several people joined in.

Helen opened the door through which Lucas had dragged the gunman. She recognised the room. This was where she had found Lucas moaning about his lost demon after his accident in Oxford Circus. The gunman was on the floor, on his side, his legs drawn up close to his chest. He was breathing. Joel Butcher came into room. Helen said, 'For god's sake, let us at least get him off the ground.' Joel moved Helen aside and with one quick heave lifted the man on to the bed.' Helen covered the man with a duvet. He said something which was incomprehensible to Helen.

'Pidgin Spanish?' Joel said.

'*Nombre?*' said Helen. But he appeared to have lost consciousness.

'Ah, the merciful English.' This was from Lucas, standing in the doorway.

'He needs a doctor,' Helen said.

'I'm sure Dr Brown will look at our friend now that she has attended to my own small needs.'

Lucas's left cheek had traces of blood.

Daugava entered the room. She was carrying a bowl of water and some cotton wool. 'Miss Berlin, tell him he must go to hospital,' she said. 'He is so obstinate, so brave.'

This presumably was the doctor. Dr Daugavia Brown, fully assimilated, at least by name.

'Perhaps you should, Mr Lucas,' Helen said.

'There is always perhaps. So perhaps tomorrow. Perhaps not at all. I have had more blood than this from shaving. Thanks to Mr Butcher I have had a scratch from a glass splinter, not a bullet in my head. No more discussion, please. Now I must comfort my poor guests.'

It was, in its way, a commanding little speech. Lucas was a presence. A thug but a presence.

Daugavia was standing by the bed. 'Swine,' she said. 'Filthy swine.' A bedside manner did not seem to be a feature of Lithuanian medicine. .

She turned to Helen and Joel. 'Leave him to me. You've done enough. Marvellous people.' Helen felt herself being ushered out of the room. She heard herself saying, 'You mustn't kill him.'

'I am a doctor, madam, a saver of life, however worthless.' She pushed Helen and Joel though the door and closed it firmly.

'I think you offended her,' Joe said.

'She offended me. Crazy women. A quack, for all we know.'

'Ah, there you are, my dears.' This from Lucas, who had apparently been saying a regretful goodbye to his guests. 'Now a glass together after this terrible evening.'

Helen was shaking her head.

'Please.'

She sat down on a sofa. 'Well, perhaps we need it.'

Lucas examined a tray of bottles and found unopened champagne. He eased off the cork carefully, covering it with a napkin.

'Enough bangs for one evening, eh, my dears?'

Cool bastard, Helen thought.

Lucas poured the drinks. 'One for you, Miss Berlin, and one for our English hero. And now may I be permitted a little ceremony? Nothing embarrassing. I know the English hate fuss.' He took from a pocket a small leather case and opened it. It contained a medal in the form of a cross, hanging from a plain maroon ribbon. 'Sulu's highest decoration for gallantry,' he said. 'But I expect you recognise it. A copy of the Victoria Cross. Some in Sulu would have preferred something of Spanish origin. But the Spanish were our oppressors. England, I said, has the best heroes. My argument prevailed.'

The medal was indeed in the shape of the Victoria Cross. But the real medal, Helen was sure, was made of bronze. It was designed to have no intrinsic value, only value as an honour. That was the point. Lucas's medal seemed to be of gold, and on each of the limbs of the cross there was embedded a large glittery thing, presumably a diamond.

'I'm very touched,' Joel said a trifle throatily as Lucas pinned the medal on a lapel of his dinner jacket. 'I've never been a hero before. All I did was jump on the chap when he pulled a gun. Sorry about the broken window.'

'Ah, you English,' Lucas said. 'What would we do without you?'

Manage with the Scots, probably, thought Helen. She was, she had worked out, one eighth Scottish.

'Now,' Lucas said, 'what do you propose to do, Miss Berlin?'

Propose? Lucas put the question as though his permission were needed before any action could be taken. Perhaps it was. Helen never felt easy in his presence.

The decision of what to do was taken out of Helen's hands with the arrival of Peter Hobbs with two officers in uniform. He was trying to stamp his authority on what seemed a puzzling assembly of strange people. The unexpected presence of Helen did not reassure him.

'Aren't you on holiday, Helen?'

'I am, Peter. It's all yours. But anything I can do, just say.'

Hobbs turned to Lucas. 'I'll arrange for your assailant to be taken away and put in custody, sir. He doesn't look as though he will run away at the moment.'

'I'm not inclined to press charges. Isn't that what you have to do in England, press charges?'

'He tried to kill you, Mr Lucas. This isn't a case of shoplifting or parking on the wrong side of the road.'

'A private matter, in a private house. I have to think of the reputation of Sulu.'

Hobbs looked at Helen, who glanced towards Joel. He returned her glance but said nothing. How stupid he looked wearing his idiotic medal.

'There is British justice,' Helen said. It was a pointless remark, but she had to say something.

'Let's get on,' Hobbs said.

'You got here quickly, Peter,' Helen said in what she hoped was a comradely tone.

'Bloody Americans,' Hobbs said irritably.

Helen had seen no American at the party. But Americans did not always wear a hat labelled Uncle Sam.

'They phoned you?'

'Yes, of course. Now let's get on'

'Anything I can do?'

'Nothing. Enjoy your holiday.'

Dismissed. Hobbs was welcome to his moment. There was much to do. Statements to be taken. Hours of work. Already people were drifting away. She had an impulse to stop them, but didn't. Don't interfere. She looked for Joel, but he was at the scene of the crime, talking to the King of Sicily. He had had a good evening.

As Helen left, Lucas put his arm around her shoulders. 'I won't forget your goodness,' he said.

SEVENTEEN

Next day Helen called on Lucas. It seemed a necessary politeness to inquire whether he had recovered from the ordeal of the party. A policeman was at the entrance of the building, but not a park copper. The apartment had been tidied. Even the smashed window had been replaced. Lucas greeted her warmly. Yes, he had charm; perhaps he no longer awed her. Each time they met the borders between them eased a little. Lucas said he would order some coffee. He pressed a bell and a woman entered the room. Helen recognised her. This was the apparent slave that she and Lucas had observed pacing the terrace of a nearby apartment. Lucas spoke to her in French. She said nothing, but gave a nod of acknowledgement and left the room.

'The woman?' Helen said.

'Farzil?' Lucas offered a look of surprise, as though there were any number of women Helen could be referring to.

'How did she get here?'

'Of her own free will, I assure you.'

'She doesn't look free. Who is she?'

'The wife of my foreign minister. I am taking care of her.'

'But you knew her when you were watching her though your binos.'

'Of course. Did I not say?'

'No.'

'You have a very western way of looking at things, Helen. It is an education for me.'
'Where's her chap, the foreign minister?'
'He has left. Defected. Gone back to Sulu.'
'Abandoned his wife?'
'It happens. But I am glad Fazil has your sympathy. I hope you will comfort her, perhaps teach her a little English. You know some French?'
'Better to find her a proper teacher.'
'You will find her intelligent,' Lucas said, as though the decision to make Helen Fazil's tutor had now been taken. 'Levantine, of course. Syrian, I believe, though she says she isn't.'
'Lebanese, I would guess.'
'How would you know?'
'I had a Lebanese friend.'
'Had one?'
'She stayed with me in London. Then back to Beirut to be closer to the Palestinians.'
'That is her cause?'
Helen nodded.
'You approved?'
'It wasn't for me to say. She believed in it.'
'What do you believe in, Helen?'
'Law and order. And myself.'
'I like you Helen.'
'That's allowed.'
'I like having you about.'
Helen felt that needed a rebuff. Keep the border intact. But she found herself smiling. She was pleased by small, silly things, like being told by your dentist that you have strong teeth or by the garage that your tyres are OK.
'You represent England for me,' Lucas said.

At the far end of the room was a large mirror. There she was, looking at herself. A portrait of England? Well, perhaps, not the England of Britannia. But something of today.

'You make me think of the finer things of life,' Lucas said. 'Like how I can become president again.'

Lucas smiled. Helen smiled too. It was not often that Lucas made a wry remark.

Lucas went to the window. Helen sensed a speech coming on.

'I should not be here, Helen. How absurd it is that when I get into difficulties I turn to foreigners for help. All my career as a politician I have praised independence, yet I need the Americans.'

'Jolly nice of them to help you. Can't think of what you could do otherwise.'

'Here I am, a mouse in a hole in London.'

'Jolly nice hole.'

'I should have turned to my people. Got them to support me.' Lucas turned from the window. 'There's still time,' he said.

Time for what? What silly notion did Lucas have now? 'You're not going back?'

'Quite soon, I think. You easily get used to inactivity, when really everything is changing, quite rapidly. At each moment of our life we assume we are going to remain stationary, but each day my enemy gets more entrenched.'

Helen had never heard Lucas mention his successor by name, only as 'the enemy' or occasionally, when Lucas was in good humour, as 'the fraud'. Presumably, 'the enemy', when speaking of Lucas, referred to him as 'the robber'.

'Of course, you will come too,' Lucas said.

Helen assumed Lucas was putting on an act. Dictators were show-offs, exotics. Look at Mussolini or Stalin. Helen was not an exotic. She liked to think of herself as an ideas person, but she accepted that original ideas were rare. She tried to give the impression that they were new in the way that ideas in magazines look new. She was as everyday as a dandelion, although a nice, fresh one. 'I take people as I find them,' was one of her expressions. She said it indignantly, as though it marked her as someone who had taken a stand against convention, when it more likely indicated a trusting nature. Lucas was not to be taken as he was found. He sometimes found it useful to look like a dandelion, an ageing one, but he worked by instinct. 'Let's try this,' he would say, with the impatience of a chess player moving a pawn beyond where it can be protected, but with the hunch that it might do some damage, if only to worry his opponent, and then see it crushed. Lucas had seen many pawns crushed.

Helen saw herself living in a fixed centre. Lucas saw himself as part of a pattern that shifted like the colours in a kaleidoscope. Each time the pattern changed he might have to make a new set of decisions and these might involve abandoning obligations and promises. But a promise was valid only at the time it was made.

Helen thought Lucas was unreliable, an obvious weakness, although it could also be said he was unpredictable, a strength. Lucas suspected Helen of being inflexible, but he felt she could offer him loyalty, a quality not much in evidence elsewhere in his life.

The coffee arrived. Helen had forgotten that Lucas had ordered it. Fazil was wearing a plastic apron over a cotton dress. She did not look like a foreign minister's wife, at a reception exchanging slightly improper *mots* across the Waterford glass. But it only took a mug shot to make a prince look like a criminal. Fazil poured some coffee and left. There were slops in Helen's saucer and the coffee tasted bitter. Perhaps she was indeed the minister's wife; she had no obvious talent as a domestic. The thought came to Helen that she might be the Mrs Lucas sometimes referred to but never seen.

The talk had turned to Lucas's visit to the National Gallery. He spoke of London's cultural abundance at the disposal of all. Helen decided not to disagree. Lucas was a dish to be taken in small bites. She was ready to leave.

'I am getting old, and cannot even start an argument,' Lucas said. 'I may as well go home and join the communists, if they will have me.'

Helen could not recall communists being mentioned in what she had learnt of Sulu's affairs since Lucas had intruded into her life.

'I thought they were extinct.'

'An endangered species, certainly. Sulu may have the largest number still in the wild. The Americans wanted to get rid of them either though bribery or slaughter. I gave them what protection I could.'

'Out of kindness?'

'Cynicism doesn't become you, Helen. Of course, there was some self-interest.'

If there were communists, Helen thought, there would be anti-communists. Lucas would have advertised his anti-communism, accepting generous amounts of aid from rich countries, much of which was quickly returned overseas into a bank account of guaranteed anonymity. Lucas would have felt that he had earned these gifts, entertaining overseas mission, putting them up in his palace, providing them with sexual partners if that was their need, arranging anti-western demos that they were able to view without any danger to themselves.

'Yes, I suppose I have to be grateful to communism. I will light a candle to their saints, Lenin, Mao, Che, Rosa, Castro, Kim.'

'And you expect them to be grateful to you?'

'The Reds would not kill me, except by accident.'

'Take you hostage. They will know about your money.'

'It is here I am a hostage. The Americans hold me in case they need me. They demand from me the new patriotism, to be anti-Islam, anti-Kyoto, and pro-Chinese, pro-globalism, pro cheap labour. Perhaps I have to break free, become a counter on the board again.'

This time Lucas would not be pushing a pawn into danger, but exposing the king. The kaleidoscope had moved a fraction, but an idea was not trivial just because it appeared to have come in a flash. Joining the communists might be the way out for Lucas that his neurons had been pondering over for weeks. He knew more about the communists in his country than almost anyone, even other communists. He knew how weak they were, even though, in order to screw money out of the democracies, he had to pretend they were strong. He would be a famous convert. They would not forgive him, but they might accept him. Lenin said little about forgiveness.

'I have always had a respect for the Reds,' Lucas said. 'It is customary to kick someone when he's down, as I have found. They had the guts to kick me when I was up.'

Oh God, Helen thought, he was serious.

'Would you come with me?'

'This is ridiculous.'

'The best ideas often seem so.'

'So do the rotten ideas.'

Lucas smiled. 'Not bad.' A pause. 'Will you think about it?'

'You are the one who should think about it.'

'I am thinking of you looking fetching in your Marxist chic, in your fighter's beret, with a bandoleer across your breasts. I am seeing brave western photographers who have trekked across the hills laden with Nikons to take your picture against the skyline. The policewoman who joined the guerrillas. I can see your memoirs displayed in the window of Hatchards, and you inside signing copies, hurriedly, because you want to get back to the Greek island you have bought with the proceeds.'

'Very well, tease me. It's still a daft idea.'

'I'm serious. The communists once turned a priest and got him to come into the hills with them. His picture appeared in newspapers all over the world. It was a magnificent coup, very embarrassing to me. People looked at it and said, well, the commies must have a case if a priest supports them, not appreciating perhaps that religion and communism often attract the same kind of person. Propaganda is a Catholic word that the communists stole.'

'I don't want to be your pin-up. It sounds dangerous.'

'Is that all?' Lucas threw his hands into the air, as though danger was the least important impediment he expected to be introduced. 'Sulu is the one of the safest places in the world. Perhaps the safest, after St James's.'

He laughed, a deep an infectious laugh of the sort kept for special occasions. Helen picked up the note and they had a laughing duet. The door opened. Fazil put her head around the door, then withdrew. Lucas came to Helen's chair, put his arms around her and kissed her on the forehead. 'Darling Helen, how I could love you were it not for Madame Lucas.'

Some while later when Helen was walking along Milkmaid's Passage, on her way to her club, she caught a glimpse in a window of herself, smiling. To Sulu with Lucas. She tried to recall the words of the conversation. She had said it was an absurd idea. So it was. But she realised that she had not actually rejected it.

EIGHTEEN

Then there was David Robinson. Perhaps she had been unfair to him. It was time to accept his plea for a talk. He would explain again that he had not been able to stop Lucas destroying her black pearl. She would forgive him, and he would be grateful. It seemed an age since they had had sex, and his testosterone must be overflowing.

There was no response when she dialled David's number. The operator said the line had been discontinued. Presumably he had not paid his bill. Just like David; it was about time he started working again. The publisher of his proposed book about Nelson suggested she try the Horatio Nelson Memorial Trust.

'Is he working there?'

'Moved in I believe.'

'What, living there?'

'So I believe.'

The trust's premises were not far from Trafalgar Square, conveniently within sight of its darling's statue. A pleasant house, late Georgian; but then, Helen thought, no other would suit.

David greeted Helen pleasantly, though not perhaps as gratefully as she had expected.

'Helen darling? What brings you here?'

Perhaps the testosterone had dried up.

Helen did not answer the question, if it was a question. She was standing in the hall underneath what looked like an admiral's hat. A notice ahead of her said, 'Please sign the visitors' register.'

'I'm glad you've found a new job, David.'

'Nelson and me, cohabitating. It sounds almost immoral. Like to see around?'

The house, Helen thought, turned out to be not all that interesting, although presumably it would be to a Nelson addict; there were portraits of the hero on every wall. The ground floor had a reception area, although no receptionist was present; on the floor above there was a large room, presumably for conferences, with an important looking table; and at the top of the house there was a small flat where David had taken up residence. More interesting was David's enthusiasm, not so much for the house itself, but for his success in taking it over. 'It was like this,' he said, and he said it frequently during the tour of the house. 'It was like this: Lucas taught me to ask for things. People are not born shy, they howl from the womb. But children are refused so often, they come to believe asking is unnatural.'

'Lucas said this?'

'He's a thoughtful fellow, you know. Full of ideas.'

'He certainly is.'

David ignored the sarcasm, or saw none. He folded his arms, the master of his universe.

'All this came from asking?'

'Lucas put me on to some Americans, uncles he calls them. I asked for a few hundred dollars to pay for another edition of my gunnery book. They seemed to be disappointed I didn't ask for more. Don't be timid, Lucas said. So I asked for enough money to keep me going while I write my Nelson book.'

'How long will that take?'

'Three years, perhaps longer. What do you think they said?'

'We love you?'

'Something like that. They said to say if I needed more.'

'So you bought this house?'
'The house is free.'
'A present from Lucas?'
'Ouch.'

Helen did feel like hitting him, and gained some minor satisfaction from having landed a verbal blow. Her idea of reconciliation with a contrite David followed by a steamy lovemaking had slipped into the realm of fantasy. All she sought to salvage from her visit was to find out how deeply David was into the thrall of Lucas. 'Sorry,' she said, 'I interrupted you.'

'The house is not really free. It belongs to the trust, of course. But I asked for permission to use its library, the best there is on Nelson. The trustees were delighted. There is not a lot of Nelsonian study these days. They insisted on providing me with a desk. Then my own office. Then I found this flat at the top was empty. It was used by the man who founded the trust and he had died. The trustees were worried that the place was empty at night, and after some dickering let me move in. I have to pay something, but not much. The uncles take care of that.'

'The uncles?'
'The Americans.'

'Oh yes,' Helen said. 'So now you are living on welfare, the dole, charity, handouts, whatever society cares to call the lilies of the field.'

'Society should look after its scholars, Lucas says.'
'No twinges of conscience?'
'Sorry?'
'I seem to remember you saying you want to compare Nelson with German war criminals. How do the trustees feel about that?'
'A scholar has to be independent.'
'Have you told them your theme?'
'Not yet.'
'Will you?'
'Eventually of course they will know.'

'And be furious?'

'Surprised, I hope, by learning about the real Nelson.'

'Bloody furious, I'd say, at being taken in.'

'A historian needs controversy. I'm not writing for the boys' book of sea heroes. I am writing about a man that today we would call a psychopath. At Copenhagen he blew the Danish fleet out of the water. He invented a new and brutal style of fighting. Before Nelson, two fleets would meet, show their flags, fire some guns, then the one that was clearly the weaker would sail away, thereby acknowledging defeat without spilling unnecessary blood. It was a gentlemanly way of conducting war. Nelson was not a gentleman. He was vulgar and popular.'

'But this German war criminal business?'

'Nelson's idea of total war came up at the trial of the German leaders at Nuremberg. The lawyers defending Admiral Doenitz argued that Germany's merciless strategy was merely a continuation of an accepted wartime practice started by Nelson. If you read a transcript of the Nuremberg proceedings, it overpowers you as you get in the grip of the terrible events being uncovered. You smell the guilt in the courthouse in Nuremberg; not just the guilt of the defendants, but the guilt of the prosecutors bound up with the illegalities of a prejudged trial. I feel guilt myself, a traitor in the house of Nelson.'

Helen felt her hostility towards Robinson receding Perhaps scholars were entitled to their own code of conduct.

'It sounds a terrific book, David. Make your name.'

'It won't though. No really. I'll get the reviews. A few weeks of controversy in the posh papers. Great. But that's all. Nelson will soon smugly resume his reputation as the greatest hero since the world began. I have to do something that will be remembered. Lucas sees that. What a perceptive man he is.'

Helen felt her hostility returning as Robinson talked of what seemed either preposterous or simply madness.

'You can see Nelson's monument from my office,' Robinson was saying. 'Not all of it. There is a building in the way. But Nelson's hat is just visible. How towering the thing must have seemed when it was put up, the closest the builders could get to putting him in Heaven. There has been nothing like it since. Churchill is at road level eternally watching the traffic lights change in Parliament Square. Other heroes are mostly no more than busts or conveniently flattened into plaques. Lucas was in my office and he said, "I wonder why no one has tried to blow it up". Well, as you can imagine, I was shocked. What good would that do? Lucas said he wasn't talking about good, but about temptation. The al-Qaeda, the Irish, the French must surely have considered it, he said. Its demolition would be a permanent statement, long outlasting formal indignation in newspaper articles and politicians' speeches. It would never be rebuilt. Plans would be made to replace it, put out to architectural competition that would be won by an Australian with a design of steel and plastic. But the plans would come to nothing. For years the boarded-up remains would continue to draw tourists. Then, sadly, someone would take the sensible decision to clear the rubble away and clean up the Landseer lions.'

'He wants you to blow up Nelson?'

'Lucas never wants. He throws out ideas.'

'Are you going barmy, David?'

'Don't worry. The column is solid. It looks fragile on a postcard, but it's made of granite. It was put up at the time when the Victorians were learning how to build to last. I hoped it might be hollow, like the Duke of York's or the Monument. Get Nelson up his arse, so to speak.'

'But you thought about it?'

'I think about many things. But yes, I've done a recce. It's a lovely place the square, too good for Nelson. Go there in the early morning, waiting with the patient pigeons for the tourists to arrive, and see how battalions of unsentimental birds close in on them like muggers. Or in the evening, watching from the porch of the National Gallery, as the rain freshens up the surface of the ponds. Did you know there are two ponds, not one, and they don't surround the monument, but adjoin it?'

Helen shook her head. Of course she did not know. But she knew that she would look next time.

'Well, I'm glad you're not going to blow it up,' she said, although she thought she sounded feeble.

'Lucas said it could be climbed from the outside, like the students who climb steeples at Oxford and put potties on the top. Lucas was at Oxford, you know?'

Helen shook her head. 'I dare say there's a lot I don't know about Lucas.'

'I suppose I shouldn't be telling you all this, you being a copper?'

'I'll put it down to fantasy, David.'

The two contemplated each other, copper and potential saboteur, lately lovers.

'Can I get you something, Helen? Cup of coffee?'

It didn't sound much of an invitation, a lousy cup of office coffee.

'I'd best be getting along.'

'No, hang on, here's Felicity, probably dying for a cup herself,' Robinson said. 'Felicity Brogan, Helen Berlin.'

The two women touched hands and constructed a silent assessment of each other.

'Felicity's giving me a hand in the office,' Robinson said. 'She worked in one of those little galleries in Bury Street. Bored to tears. But loved Patrick O'Brian. Did you ever get around to Aubrey and Maturin, Helen?'

The question did not seem to require an answer. Robinson was trying to fill an empty space.

'Keep in touch,' Helen said. A useful English phrase, politely dismissive. As she walked away, she consoled herself that there were worse things in life than not having sex, although that could be a matter of dispute.

NINETEEN

Helen arrived at her parents' house in Kent with a bag of books for holiday reading, but she felt no inclination to open it. She sat on the verandah of the house warmed by the early spring sunshine, dozing until disturbed by a movement behind her.
 'Daddy?'
 'Sorry, Helen. I thought you were asleep.'
 'Thinking, Daddy. Not asleep at all.'
 Her father was carrying a phone, with one hand protectively, but pointlessly, over the mouthpiece.
 'For me?'
 'Chap called Hobbs. Says he is from the Yard.'
 Helen took the phone. 'What's up, Peter?'
 'You been asleep, Helen? I've been trying to get you all morning.'
 'Thinking, Peter. I do that sometimes.'
 'Your dad said you were asleep.'
 'Get to the point, Peter. Or did you just want a friendly chat?'
 'It's about Lucas.'
 'Ah.'
 'Does he sometimes go out a bit without telling anyone?'
 'You've lost him, Peter?'
 'I haven't lost anyone. But he wasn't in when I called at his flat. Just this foreign woman, a maid I suppose, who doesn't know much English.'
 'There's a park copper who keeps an eye on the place.'

'He didn't see Lucas. But then he didn't come on until nine. Is Lucas in the habit of taking an early stroll?'

Helen did not answer the question. She was already several light years ahead of Peter Hobbs' plodding mind

'Are you sure Lucas isn't still in the flat?'

'That's a point. Awkward sort of bugger.'

'You could say that.'

'That may be the answer then?'

Helen sensed a sigh of relief coming down the phone line.

'Maybe, maybe not. What does Jenkins say?'

'He said to phone you, get a picture of Lucas's habits. Didn't he go off before, have an accident in Oxford?'

'Oxford Circus. Peter, shall I come up, give you a hand?'

'And a pretty little hand it would be, Helen. No, everything's under control. I reckon the bugger's holed up in that mansion.'

Helen resisted a sharp response. Being patronised wasn't the worst hazard she had encountered at the Yard.

'Well, the offer's there, Peter. You might have a chat with Carruthers Smith at the Foreign Office. He knows a lot about Lucas's background.'

'Carruthers? How do you spell that?'

Helen spelt the name, slowly.

'And there's an American general,' Peter said. 'Ripley? Believe it or not?'

'Sorry?'

'Ripley. Believe it or Not. Cartoon series. Before your time, I expect.'

Before her time. How old was Hobbs? Quite old.

'You spoke to him?'

'Jenkins did. That's how I came to Lucas's place. Sorry if I was a bit short with you.'

'I was relieved to see you. The cavalry arrived just in time.'

'Sometimes a bit of experience helps, Helen.'

Helen denied herself a retort. Respect the aged.

'Well, call me if I can do anything.'
'No problem. I'll find the rascal.'

But he wouldn't. Helen thought. Where was he? In Sulu for all she knew. She switched off the phone and took it to the kitchen and replaced it in its holder on the wall. Her mother was at the stove.

'Mummy, should you be up?'

Her mother was in her dressing gown but, Helen noticed, was wearing shoes; dressed for bed, but possibly equipped for an excursion outdoors of a limited nature.

'I was desperate for a coffee.'

'You should have asked Bessie.'

'She has too much to do. Anyway, she always makes it too weak. Now I will join you outside and you can tell me terrible stories of criminal gangs.'

She carried two cups out to the verandah. Helen fetched a chair and placed it next to her own. She took one of the cups, examined the black sludge inside and put it aside for quiet disposal later. Her mother said, 'This is so nice. But how can they spare you with all this crime going on?'

'Bit of leave before I move up.'

'Just remind me, what are you now? Corporal?'

'Just a constable.'

'A private?'

'That sort of thing.'

'When I first knew your father he was a private, then a lance corporal, then a corporal, then a sergeant. It was so exciting, every letter he seemed to get another stripe. And then of course he became an officer.' She began listing the officer ranks. 'Second lieutenant, then …'

She had a good memory for the distant past, Helen thought; a bit blurry about the present. She supposed that was normal for her age, whatever normal was. Was it normal to spend much of her life in bed, with occasional expeditions downstairs? She refused to see a doctor. She was not ill, she said, and anyway doctors were busy. On a previous visit Helen had insisted that she see a doctor, threatening never to come home to Kent ever again if she refused. It had been a foolish thing to say, and her mother had called her bluff, making Helen feel like an impertinent child. It was her choice to arrange her life around bed. It was a luxury her body was entitled to after doing its duty bearing and rearing four children, five if you counted the miscarriage.

Helen's mother was up to the rank of colonel. 'Still, you've made a good start, Helen. Corporal next, I expect.'

'It's a different system in the police.'

'In wartime promotion was quicker, but Daddy doesn't like to be told that.' She laughed, quite loudly.

'Did I hear someone talking about me?'

Helen's father was on the verandah, in his Barbour jacket.

'Just off to my appointment,' he said.

'Pick up my Mozart, would you dear?'

When he had gone, Helen sought to decode the exchange. The Mozart was presumably a recording her mother had ordered in Tunbridge Wells, a nearby town. What her father's appointment might be she had no idea.

'Poor Daddy,' her mother said. 'It's taking so long.'

'Sorry?'

'The pulled muscle. Didn't he tell you?'

'No.'

'He never complains. We are two of a kind.'

'He is having treatment for muscle pain?'

'Didn't he tell you?'

Helen could not recall her father mentioning any pain. Nor did he seem to be handicapped in any way. He was remarkably active about the house and took long walks.

'He's having some physio?' Helen said.

'What was that, dear?'

'Physiotherapy. Massage.'

'A massage person, that's right.'

'You've met this person?'

'Of course I haven't. Nothing wrong with my muscles. Why all the questions?'

'I worry about Daddy, as I worry about you.'

'Of course you do. But Daddy says she is a very kind and thoughtful, and it hardly hurts at all. So I don't worry, and you need not worry either.'

Helen examined her mother's face for some coy hint of a secret too adult to be shared with a child. But it offered no message.

'All this talking,' she said. 'I feel quite tired.'

Helen followed her to her bedroom. This was furnished primarily to allow her mother to realise a number of ambitions. She said she would hate to die without speaking another language well, without seeing all of Shakespeare, reading some Greek philosophy, the whole of the Bible, knowing more of Mozart and much more about the rest of music, especially early music. So the bedroom contained many books, tidily arranged on shelves, together with a large-screen television and good quality recording equipment. She was cross that she had left many important things so late, which, Helen thought, was what most people felt, at whatever age they died. The problems of those who were going to survive her had ceased to concern her mother. Dying was her full-time occupation. She had detached herself from anything bothersome. She was attentive towards her grown-up children when they came to her bedside, but she no longer tried to order their lives. Her answer to any request involving a decision was to leave it to Daddy. 'You know how much he loves you. And now, my darlings, I must rest, and perhaps listen to some music. You must come again very soon.'

'And now, my darling, I must rest,' she said to Helen. 'Daddy will be back soon. I am sure he will have lots to tell you.'

'I'm sorry to hear about your muscle problem, Dad,' Helen said invitingly at lunch.

'Oh, your mother. She always fusses about things.' The response said nothing, unless it was that her father was not going to disclose any details of his adventure to his daughter. If in fact he was having an adventure. Helen thought it kinder not to pursue the matter, although she was intrigued that there might be a massage parlour with dirty dollies in Tunbridge Wells, and that her father might patronise their services. He was, she supposed, what was known as 'well preserved' for his age, more perhaps than Lucas was. Lucas would be younger but his face, Helen thought, had not worn well, perhaps because of all the nasty things he had done. Every face, however imperturbable it seems, is a catalogue of information.

'You are looking at me,' her father said.

'With affection, Daddy. As always.'

'You are thinking of something. What was that man Hobbs on about? This Lucas business?'

'Peter Hobbs. Lucas is eluding him.'

'I met Lucas once, you know?'

'No, I didn't know that.'

'He was in London on some jaunt, and was sent round to me with toothache.'

Helen's father had been a dentist.

'And you fixed it?'

'The tooth could be saved, but that would have meant two visits. He opted for an extraction, get it over with. Nor would he have an anaesthetic.'

'Brutal.'

'I did my best.'

'Painful, I mean.'

'Some people can take a lot of pain. It's not brave. Just the way they are.'

'And can cause pain?'

'I don't think he was a sadist. I quite liked him. He offered me a job.'

Helen smiled.

'What's so funny?' he father said.

'He is still offering people jobs. It must be habit.'

'I thought about taking it. Sunny Sulu.'

'Lots of money?'

'Decent pay, I suppose. But it was the power that tempted me.'

Power? Helen contemplated her father, now sitting back in his chair having eaten most of a pasta dish that Bessie was clearing away, the dependable parent in seemingly contented retirement, but secretly lusting after women in massage parlours and regretting that he did not work for a dictator. It was enough to make a daughter feel she hardly knew her father at all.

'I see you smiling again, Helen. But in those days Sulu was not a dictatorship. Lucas had been elected democratically. It was only later he scrapped elections. He had great plans for setting up a health service free for all, the first of its kind in Asia. I was to be its director, its creator in practical terms. There was nothing comparable in Britain for me.'

'So why didn't you take it?'

'Inertia, I suppose. Moving a young family to the unknown.'

'Did Lucas ever set up this health dream?'

'No.'

'Good thing you stayed put, then'

'Not so good for Sulu, perhaps, or for Lucas.'

'You would have made a difference?'

'Certainly.'

Helen was surprised by the strength of her father's conviction. Her guess was that Lucas's health scheme had been a passing fancy.

'I wouldn't have let him, you see?' her father said. Bessie leaned across the table to take his tumbler, but he held on to it and refilled it with water. This was serious talk. 'You may think Lucas is interested only in money, but power is his drug, as was Hitler's and Stalin's. They died penniless. Why bother with money when your every request is obeyed, if not anticipated? Lucas has this thing he said to people. "I can make you rich", but money had no use for him unless it gave him power. I would have said to him, "I will make you more powerful." He couldn't have resisted it. I should have done it. I still could.'

Helen looked with affection at her father, fantasising in his second childhood, or his third. It seemed unlikely that he had considered giving up his profitable dental practice in London for a job in an unhealthy tropical dump, but now he could imagine doing so, in a state of virtual reality, bereft of danger. Perhaps this is what he thought of as the massage parlour girl attended to his muscle.

Her father was refilling his glass again but any further talk was interrupted by Bessie.

'Man at the door,' she said to Helen.

A diagonal shadow across the porch transformed into a man in chauffeur's uniform. He handed Helen an envelope. The message inside said, 'Miss Berlin, Please come in this car to see me. It is important. You will not be in any danger. Lucas.'

'Where is Mr Lucas?'

'I'm just the driver, miss.'

'But you have seen him?'

'No miss, I was told to give you the letter and bring you to London.'

'Now?'

'If you are ready, miss.'

Helen's father was standing behind her. He read the letter. 'Just when we were having an interesting chat,' he said.

'I suppose I should go?' She looked at her father and then at the driver. Her father offered a smile.

Helen said goodbye to her mother, picked up her bag of books and her overnight bag, which she had not unpacked. 'I'll come back tonight, if there's a train,' she told her father. 'Tomorrow at the latest.'

The car had darkened windows, so until Helen was inside she was unaware that she had a companion for the journey, a woman she had met previously. She hunted for the name. Dugavia. Dr Dugavia Brown. She of Lucas's party.

'Helen, my dear.' Dugavia held out a hand. 'I apologise for not coming to the door. We are a bit pushed for time. Have you eaten? I packed a few refreshments.'

Helen said she had just had lunch.

'Perhaps later, then.'

'But we are not going far?'

'Not too far.'

'London, the driver said.'

'Yes, I expect so.'

Helen said, 'I've changed my mind. I'd like to go back.'

'I am afraid that would be difficult, Helen. We are a little behind time. Your house was not all that easy to find.'

'You are abducting me?'

'That's very melodramatic, Helen. You are in no danger. You have the president's word. Sit back. Be comfortable. We can talk. Or there is music, a disc-player. Or just close your eyes.'

Helen said nothing. She was thinking what an idiotic, stupid, ridiculous, moronic fool she had been. She had not made the simplest checks. Now she had to wake up. She started to observe the route the car was taking. So far it was familiar territory, known to her since childhood.

'I am afraid I must ask you to wear a blindfold,' Dugavia said.

'Why is that?'

'The president wants to keep his whereabouts confidential. It is really for your protection.'

'I can't see anything anyway. These dark windows.'

'Just to be safe.'

'I'd rather not.'

'Don't make me insist, Helen.'

Dugavia presumably had prepared for non-co-operation with something nastily medical.

'Well, I hope it won't be for long.'

'That's good of you, Helen. I do appreciate it.'

Helen felt her head being covered by what seemed to be a hood of some kind, perhaps of silk.

'There,' Dugavia said. 'That's not so bad, is it?'

'Terrible. Pull the mouth hole down a bit so I can breathe.'

'There. Now you look like a Muslim girl. Watch out for randy sheikhs.'

'I'm not in a joking mood.'

'You've been marvellous. Now I just want you to give me your hands.'

Helen felt handcuffs being placed on her wrists. She tried to lift her hands, but the cuffs seemed to have been fastened to the seat.

'Now just relax, Helen. What about some music? Do you like Stacey Kent?'

TWENTY

Lucas said, 'You can go, of course.'
'Just walk out?'
'The car is at your disposal. It will take you back to your parents, or to your flat in London. Or wherever. I am not a kidnapper.'
Helen made a gesture of rubbing her wrists.
'A little harmless restraint,' Lucas said. 'I would not call your journey suffering, apart perhaps from having Dugavia for company. Better for us to have met again in a less dramatic way but, as I have tried to explain, I am in a sense a prisoner here.'
Helen and Lucas had been talking for two hours, perhaps a little longer; anyway, ever since her arrival. At first she felt both furious and foolish. As those two conditions abated they were replaced by curiosity. During this time, a picture had emerged of Lucas's adventures since she had last seen him.
Lucas had been hurt, more than Helen had realised at the time, that no one from the American embassy, not even an office boy, had attended his party. It was worse than being ignored; it was humiliation in front of his friends. Lucas described the meeting he had had with the American at the Ritz. He told it well, she thought, mimicking the American's voice convincingly. But she restrained herself from applauding. To be an attentive listener, she thought, was sufficient reward for Lucas. Presumably there was more to come. How did Lucas get from the Ritz to here? Anyway, where was here? Through her hood she had listened for

sounds that might indicate where she was being taken. Towards the end of the journey she had heard the noise of an aircraft, quite close and loud. While Lucas was talking there had been the occasional noise of an aircraft taking off or landing. Now she heard an aircraft approaching, from very quiet to very loud and presumably very low, so that the building vibrated.

'There is a runway nearby,' Lucas said.

'I worked that out for myself. Can I be told the name of the airport?'

'We are in an American military base, I think in eastern England. I was brought here yesterday.'

'Brought here?'

'For my own protection, I was told.'

'General Ripley?'

'You know him?'

Helen smiled faintly at Lucas's expression of surprise.

'He's been nagging the police. After the attack at your party.'

'I see,' Lucas said, but he did not sound as though he did.

'And why am I here?' Helen said. 'For my own protection?'

'I wanted to see you. Someone I could trust. An honest person. A rarity in my experience.'

It was not unpleasant, Helen thought, to be called honest, a rarity, even though this wholesome reputation was based on a misunderstanding: Lucas's belief that she had rejected the black pearl on moral grounds when really she had lusted after it and was furious when Robinson reported that it had been destroyed.

'Why not just phone me, instead of all this cloak and dagger stuff?'

'The Americans. No outside contact, they said.'

'But now I am here.'

'As a special favour. This is difficult, Helen. I said I needed a sexual companion who would be brought here secretly. The Americans smirked and said okay. I apologise. Naturally, I respect you in every way.'

'Like trussing me up?'

'That was Dugavia's idea. To get you through the gates.'

'I was trussed up the whole journey.'

'She has nasty tendencies, Helen. But I have sent her away.'

'Won't she make a fuss about you being here?'

'She is in the pay of the Americans. She tipped off Ripley about the best time to grab me.'

'So you are a prisoner?'

'In a sense.'

'But I can go?'

'I think there would be no problem.'

'You'd have finished with the tart's services?'

'You make me feel ashamed.'

Was it possible to feel sorry for Lucas, dictator and probable murderer? He was in a low state. It was probably the first time in his life that he had been locked up, as presumably he was here. In Sulu he had presumably experienced a sort of confinement, as endured by all heads of state, considered too precious to be allowed out on their own in case some lunatic took a shot at them. But he would have had the illusion of personal freedom. In London, he was confined by his ignorance of the local district, but he was gradually venturing beyond his front door. Helen wondering how long the Americans proposed to keep Lucas on the base. Probably they had no idea. They just wanted to put him in a safety deposit until, or if, they needed him. And suppose they did not need him? Would he be returned to his flat? Perhaps not. He would not only be redundant; he could be a nuisance. These thoughts would presumably now be going though Lucas's mind. Lucas would know what to do with a nuisance. He would arrange for him to be killed. Would be believe the Americans would do otherwise? No wonder Lucas felt low, and sought someone he believed trustworthy he could talk to. But Helen was not a nursemaid. That may have been how Carruthers Smith had seen her when she had reported for duty at the Foreign Office at what now seemed a long time ago. Her nursemaid job had been terminated. Did she feel sorry for Lucas? Yes, a bit. Should she hang about to comfort him in his misery? Hardly. However, professionally she remained on duty as a police officer. A man had almost certainly been killed in Lucas's flat, and Lucas had almost certainly been the killer. At the Yard the file on the man's body remained open, the case unsolved. The Yard liked its cases to be solved; the files closed. But for reasons concerned with the strange world of diplomacy, Lucas had never been questioned about the case. Helen had no authority to question him now. But supposing Lucas cared voluntarily to make a statement to Helen? Was that likely? No. A possibility? Still probably no. A chance? Well, there was always a chance. The most mystifying cases were sometimes cleared up by chance.

'What sort of accommodation have they given you here?' she said.

'Look around.'

Lucas had been provided with what amounted to a largish suite of a type to be found in a modern hotel. There was the lounge, where Helen and Lucas had been talking. Leading off it Lucas had a large impersonal bedroom with a large bed and a bathroom. Next to it was another bedroom.

'The tart's room?' Helen said.

Lucas said nothing.

She looked inside. It was a slightly smaller replica of Lucas's room, again with its own bathroom.

Through a third door there was a small kitchen.

'Who does the cooking?'

'The food arrives.'

'Room service?'

'That sort of thing.'

'Any good?'

'American food. Made in factories.'

'How long were you expecting me to stay?'

Lucas did not reply for perhaps half a minute. Then he said, 'I'd have not been surprised if you had demanded to return the moment you were brought here. You have been patient and thoughtful, listening to my woes. I've been lucky.'

Helen looked at her watch. It was now early evening. 'I must be off tomorrow.'

Lucas half bowed. 'More than I deserve.'

'Perhaps you could get a real tart in?'

'It is not a problem.'

Did Lucas mean that there was no difficulty obtaining a tart, or that he had no sexual needs? Helen did not pursue the question. She said, 'What time is dinner?'

'Prisoners here have the luxury of ordering food at any time. It could become a dangerous habit. Would about seven-thirty suit you?'

'Candlelight at seven-thirty: what could be nicer?'

Lucas took a card from a desk drawer and handed it to Helen.

'The menu,' Helen murmured. 'Just like a real hotel.'

Various cuts of steak were on offer, together with varieties of pasta and a number of dishes described as "quickie bites", mainly hamburgers.

'Looks like steak,' she said. 'Fillet if they have it. Medium done.'

She handed the card to Lucas who studied it, unusually carefully, she thought, as presumably he had seen it before.

'A good choice,' he said. 'The Americans will approve.'

'Perhaps I'll have the pasta, then.'

'You've changed your mind?'

'Of course not. I thought you were making a joke.'

'I lack your English sense of humour. But so, I suspect, do the Americans.'

'You mean they care whether you have steak or not?'

'Steak is American. Pasta is not.'

'You think they keep a dossier on what you eat?'

'A record, yes. Is that so unlikely?'

'It is bloody ridiculous. Are they getting you down?'

Lucas said nothing. He picked up the phone and gave instructions for their meal.

'Now, Helen,' he said, 'if you will excuse me. I like to have a short rest before dinner.'

Helen entered her own room. She tried the shower. It was invitingly hot and powerful, and scoured her body with the efficiency of a car-wash. Americans were good with showers.

She opened her bag. She had packed frugally for her visit to her parents, but it contained one item, a white silk blouse, that might pass for evening wear. She told herself that she was not aiming to please Lucas. She simply wanted to wear something clean. Lucas would perhaps notice that she had gone to the trouble to change, and would take it as a sign of politeness, the famous English politeness, nothing more. The blouse was of a style that buttoned to the neck. Helen held a brooch against the top button and studied the effect in a mirror. Too severe, she thought, the policewoman's night out. She undid the top button and the button below that. Was the effect too casual? A sweet disorder in the dress. Herrick was unfamiliar with the etiquette of dining with a dictator at an American base, but had he been he might have hinted at the danger of encouraging lust. Lucas had not shown any obvious signs of lust, only of domination. Perhaps there was a link. Helen was not wholly convinced that Dugavia had acted on her own in the antics in the car. Lucas had made her a prisoner, albeit briefly, on her first visit to his flat. Had she been foolhardy in agreeing to stay overnight in this apartment? Well, the decision had been taken. She would lock her door before going to bed and put a chair against the handle. Now there was the evening to be faced. She put on some make-up, and had a final look in the mirror at Lucas's companion for the evening. From top to bottom, the silk blouse with one button undone, a black belt, and a denim skirt to below the knee. Versace might not have been impressed, but she had made a gesture.

Lucas was reading the *Stars and Stripes* when Helen came into the lounge. She noted that he too had made a gesture to the evening, and had put on a dark jacket instead of the cardigan he had been wearing earlier. He put aside the newspaper, stood and slowly moved towards Helen. He held her shoulders and kissed her left cheek, softly. He stepped back two paces.

'How very thoughtful you are,' he said. He studied Helen for what seemed an age, though it was probably no more than half a minute. He seemed to linger over her shoes.

They were not evening shoes, but they were the only ones she had with her. They were more boots than shoes. They encased the leg to just above the ankle. A neat but efficient zip disciplined the leather to follow the shape of the foot without a wrinkle. The woman who had served Helen in a Venetian boutique called them a masterpiece, an object that Titian would loved to have painted. They had the *andrigino* of conventional boots but without their discomfort. They would provide Helen with many conquests, she said.

Helen had no ambition to conquer Lucas, far from it. All the same, it was pleasant to be admired. Although Helen had worn the shoes since that morning, they had retained their dignity. Helen's father, who had been cleaning her shoes since she wore Startrites, had given them a thorough polish. Helen rubbed them against a sofa. 'There,' she said. 'Good as new.' A pause, then she said, 'Now to practical matters. Do you want me to disappear when the food is delivered?'

'It will come on a trolley, with two attendants, GIs, who will lay the table. They are pleasant young men, who make a few conventional remarks, and work quickly. Their task will be finished in a few minutes. I do not think they will embarrass you, but you may feel more comfortable in dark glasses.' Lucas took a pair of shades from a pocket inside his jacket. 'I sometimes wear them myself.'

Helen put them on. She could see a reflection of herself in a window of the lounge. She thought she resembled a gangster's moll. Well, look the part. It was the best disguise.

The couple that delivered the food were a man and a woman. Helen thought the woman gave her a careful look, but endeavoured to be discreet. Otherwise the ceremony was as Lucas had predicted. When the attendants had left Lucas examined the arrangement, lifting the covers on the hot dishes.

'All correct, Mr President?' Helen said.

'The champagne is an extra, if it is champagne.' He lifted the bottle from its bucket. 'Californian.' He crunched the bottle deep into its cushion of ice. 'The colder the better, I suspect.' Lucas surveyed the table again. 'And flowers. You are good for me.'

'Any time, Mr President.'

Lucas said nothing, and Helen wondered if she was taking mockery too far.

'No offence intended.'

'Certainly none taken. I have now been in England long enough to understand your famous sense of humour. Can I say though that I like being called Mr President, even if you say it in jest? But I am afraid that makes me sound foolish and weak.'

Lucas was so waiting for a denial that Helen heard herself saying, 'Not at all. Perfectly reasonable.'

'Now, Helen, what would be the top rank you could achieve in the police?'

'I hope soon to be a sergeant.'

'But higher than that, much higher?'

'Superintendent, commander. Not very likely though.'

'Commander Helen and Mr President. Let us make those our roles for the evening.'

Role playing sounded like an intimacy, but a harmless one. Lots of people still probably thought of Lucas as a president.

'If it pleases you.' A pause. 'Mr President.'

'Thank you, Commander Helen. Now shall we eat?'

The steak, Helen thought, was good, and generous in size. She decided she must be hungry. Lucas opened the champagne expertly, with hardly a pop. She sipped her glass and thought of sunlight on frost. This wasn't such a bad evening. She asked Lucas if he remembered offering her father a job.

'What does he do?'

'Did. He was a dentist. You had toothache. Emergency.'

'Then I should remember. Berlin? The name should register, Commander Helen. Your father didn't change his name?'

'No.'

'It was a long time ago?'

'Of course.'

'Perhaps I will recall his name later. The memory has a poor filing system. What job does he say I offered him?'

'To start a free health service in Sulu.'

'Then I should certainly have remembered him. Tell me, commander, what did your father think of this idea?'

'Very favourably,' Helen said, then added quickly, 'Mr President'.

'He turned it down?'

'He was doing well in London and did not want to give up his practice.'

Lucas leaned across the table and refilled Helen's glass. 'But he was pleased to be offered this opportunity?'

'Who wouldn't be?'

'He thought well of me?'

Helen tried to remember exactly what her father had said about Lucas. He was not hostile, but nor was he a fan. But that was not what Lucas wanted to hear.'

'Obviously he liked you.'

'Did he? That is very charming.' Lucas seemed to ponder over this presumably welcome disclosure of her father's feelings towards the dictator, and she wondered if he would take the risk of asking her if she liked him too, and what on earth she would say. But Lucas seemed to be satisfied with one vote of approval.

'Daddy said you weren't a dictator then.'

'Yes I had the votes. In some places more people voted than there were voters. But that was always a foible of the system. People shrugged and said that the birds must have voted this year, and perhaps even the flowers. But my opponent canvassed the birds too, so there was some fairish cancelling out in the result. I was the ablest man, and I won. Nothing wrong in that. A picture was taken of me leaving the building where I had been voted president. I am bounding forward, one arm raised and pointing to the sun.'

Lucas raised an arm and pointed to the ceiling.

'Walking on air, if I may be allowed a banality. If Fred Astaire had been elected president, this is how he would have expressed his utter triumph. You have heard of Astaire?'

Helen nodded, smiling.

'I adored that picture. Don't know why I left it behind.'

'There must be a copy,' Helen said.

'You really think so?'

'Was it printed in the Sulu newspapers?'

'Many times.'

'There you are. Easy.'

'You will get one for me?'

Helen had not intended to imply that, but she said, 'If I can.'

'You'd have liked me then, Helen. Youth is short. It is life that is long.'

Helen was not going to say that she liked him now, although that presumably was what he was after. He had charmed her to the extent that she found she did not dislike him. At least he seemed to have dropped the commander business.

'I did not rob the poor, whatever my enemies say. Sometimes I would declare an amnesty for troublesome prisoners. But it is not easy to introduce benevolence into dictatorship. My lieutenants would say, "Is this a good idea, Mr President?" And of course it wasn't.'

Lucas packed the detritus of dinner on to the trolley and pushed it out of the apartment. 'The elves will do the washing up.'

He suggested they watch television. Helen wondered what was on.

'It is of no consequence,' Lucas said. 'All television is the same. I like its parochialism, its obsession with its own tiny bit of the world, limited to how far the transmission can reach. Only once have I seen my country mentioned and that was by an Englishman who had been there in the 1930s.'

Lucas clicked through half a dozen stations so rapidly that none was offered a chance to make its pitch. He finished with a blank screen.

'It gets better as the night goes on,' he said, 'when the participants become wordier and wilder, like children who have been allowed to stay up while the grown-ups have gone to bed. But even the children get weary, and sometimes I feel I may be the only watcher.'

Helen glanced at her watch; not obviously, but Lucas noticed the movement.

'You are right, Commander Helen. Let us not spoil a lovely evening by stretching it beyond its natural length.'

'I have some reading to do,' Helen said. 'Catching up.'

'Of course you have.' He got up. Helen got up. 'I prepare my own breakfast in the little kitchen. Just coffee usually, although a bag of croissants and some fresh bread is left outside the door.'

He leaned towards Helen and delivered a brush on her cheek. Then he was gone into his room.

So that was all. Not even a grope. Did she feel a sigh of relief, a metaphorical sheathing of her nail file? Emptiness, really, and a discovery of how anxious she had been.

She entered her room, undressed and had a shower. In bed, she started to read. A sound disturbed her, a snuffling. She wondered if there was an animal in her room, a pet. Improbable but, goodness knows, possible. She put aside her book and got out of bed. She looked in the wardrobe. Empty except for the clothes she had been wearing that evening and which she had optimistically put on hangers, hoping that their creases would shake out. There was nowhere else in the room where an animal might be hiding. She opened the bedroom door, which she had neither locked nor put a chair against. The snuffling voice was louder. She put an ear to the door of Lucas's room.

'Are you all right in there?'

No answer.

She opened the door slightly, as though a modest peep would not be considered an intrusion.

Her first thought was that Lucas was ill. Possibly he had had a seizure of some kind. But the details Helen almost immediately took in did not support that diagnosis. He was lying on his back on his bed, unclothed. In his right hand he held a condom, in his left his penis, which seemed to be in a limp state.

Helen withdrew her head, and sought to close the door softly.

'Helen?'

'Sorry, I thought I heard a noise.'

'So you did. From a poor old fool who doesn't know his age.'

Helen came into the room. Her knowledge of penises was not extensive but she had had enough experience of them to know their mechanics was not always reliable. Robinson's penis had been shy, although in other ways he had been attentive. She remembered a prostitute had once told her that thirty-five percent of her clients had difficulty achieving an erection, and of this number some fifty percent were young men. When Helen showed surprise the woman politely pointed out that she was an expert. She saw a dozen penises a day, more than a doctor saw in a month. But Helen was not surprised by her expertise, only by the accountancy. No doubt, Helen had suggested, this high rate of failure was a disappointment? It was a challenge, the woman said, but as a therapist she did not give up. What sort of therapy?

Use your imagination, the woman had said. She was not inclined to disclose any more professional information to a copper.

Lucas's penis was clearly among the thirty-five per cent. Yet clearly he had not despaired of it, despite being among the fifty percent who were no longer young. Helen returned to her room and found her shoes that had ambitions to be boots. She sniffed them. A blend of animal skin, polish and sweat.

'What are you doing?' Lucas said when she returned. He was sitting up.

'Lie back. This is something that Englishmen like.'

She put a shoe against Lucas's lips.

'Kiss it and think of me.'

Helen held Lucas's penis and watched it grow rapidly, like a plant on a nature programme on television that expands instantly though trick photography. But she wasn't thinking of nature photography. She thought of an old car whose engine suddenly fires triumphantly after some fiddling under the bonnet.

'That's more like a presidential prick,' she said.

She rolled the condom on to the penis.

'There. Gift wrapped. Time for you to do the male thing.'

Lucas put his arms around Helen and sought to move into the position unfairly named after missionaries. But what might have been a simple exercise seemed to be undermined by the softness of the bed. Helen had not previously thought of Lucas as being other than fit. Now he looked flabby, even weak, as though by removing his clothes he had been deprived of essential support. Helen gently removed his arms and eased him back. Having got the old car to start, it would have been a wasted labour if now it faltered. She reached for the shoe, but testosterone had taken over and Lucas was on auto.

The worst that could happen now, Helen thought, was that Lucas would have a heart attack. Would the Americans want a clapped-out Lucas? It was impossible to say. Roosevelt and Kennedy had both been cripples. There were days when Bush did not look too good. Were great issues of Asian politics being determined? Perhaps not. Lucas had come, and remained conscious.

'What about you?' he said. A kindly concern for a dictator, Helen thought.

'I'm content,' she said.

TWENTY-ONE

Helen was awakened by a knock on her bedroom door. She got up and released the door catch, which for some reason she had fastened, despite the intimacies of the previous evening.

'Breakfast time,' Lucas said. He wheeled in a trolley, similar to the one that had carried their dinner, but this time bearing coffee, rolls and two boiled eggs.

'I'll come out,' Helen said.

'There's a maid cleaning the room. I thought you'd prefer privacy.'

It was not a totally unfamiliar experience for Helen to have breakfast in a strange bedroom with a man she had not long met, although she would not say she made a habit of it. In a single generation the chaste romance of the black and white movie had been replaced by cheerful promiscuity. But that in turn had been modified by caution. Helen was careful about free-range sex. Why she had attended to Lucas's needs remained unclear to her. But the events of the night should not have to be answerable to questions posed in the daylight of the morning.

'Now then, Helen, the programme for the day.'

Lucas had manoeuvred the breakfast trolley to the side of the bed, where Helen was now sitting. Lucas was opposite her on a chair and was pouring coffee. He appeared to have regained confidence, perhaps, Helen thought, because he was wearing clothes again.

Helen said she had her own programme for the day. It was to go home.

'And so you shall,' Lucas said. 'A presidential promise. I have to say, though, there has to be a slight delay, a few hours only, the morning at the most.'

'What sort of delay?'

'I have to get your passport cleared.'

'Passport?'

'American bureaucracy. Terrible.'

'I can't get out without a passport?'

'In or out. But you got in without one. That's the problem.'

'Is this a ploy to keep me here?'

'Ploy? An English word, I suspect?'

'Plan, plot. You know what I mean.'

'You must trust me, Helen. You will away by lunchtime. I promise. Is that so unreasonable?'

'Do I have a choice?'

'I take that to mean you agree. I am grateful. It will not, I think, be an uninteresting time for you. I personally will be seeing some Americans. Political people. So we cannot spend the morning together. However, I have arranged for you to be given a tour of the base.'

'I can't wait.'

'You scoff, Helen.'

Helen said nothing; she smiled, she hoped enigmatically. In fact she was relieved that the morning promised merely boredom, rather than a rerun of the previous evening's pantomime.

Lucas said, 'Better not say you are in the police.'

'Better an ordinary tart?'

'If you must use that word. Ordinary, if you like. Certainly not hostile. The Americans are simple people. You are a visiting friend. If they learn you are in the police they will be confused. Why would I be visited by the police? Was I up to something they did not understand?'

'Supposing I bump into General Ripley?'

'There are several thousand people on this base. Few of them will know of you. Most of the time you will be in a car. Bumping, I hope, is not very likely.'

'But dark glasses, perhaps?'

'If you wish.'

When Helen emerged from the suite she was wearing shades and bright lipstick. She had decided to look the part as far as resources would allow.

A mini-bus was waiting for her. It had a left-hand drive. Two people were already inside, the driver who presumably was also the guide and a man who had a large briefcase and looked like a civil servant. Both greeted her courteously, perhaps over-courteously, but the driver looked too young for sex, and the civil servant too old.

'Welcome to RAF Honeysucklelay,' the driver said.

'This is an RAF station?'

'RAF Honeysucklelay, ma'am.'

'The Royal Air Force?'

'Sorry, ma'am?'

'Never mind. I was a bit confused. Please carry on.'

'Perhaps I may help.' Four nicely articulated words from the man who looked like a civil servant. 'It is formally an RAF base. The Americans are our guests. That right Joe?'

'Thank you, your grace.'

Helen took off her shades. The gesture implied a question.

'Joe is a flatterer. I fear I am not a duke.' He held out a hand. 'I answer to Johnny.'

'Helen.'

'Good,' said Johnny who was not a duke, but spoke like one. 'Now we are properly introduced. Helen, Joe and Johnny. We sound like one of those pop groups that make millions of pounds. Forward, Joe. Let's fly away, in the words of Sinatra.'

'You want some music, your grace?'

'I think not. Helen?'

'No.'

'I think that is unanimous. We are entirely in your hands, Joe.'

Joe reached into a pocket beside the dashboard and produced a small flattish stone, which he handed to Helen.

'What do you think that is, ma'am?'

Helen recognised it as part of a flint tool, or possibly an arrowhead. Probably Neolithic. A short course on archaeology she had once signed up to on impulse had not been wasted.

'Just a bit of stone, eh ma'am?'

Helen observed Joe's eager, boyish face, bursting with information. She handed back the flint. 'That's what it looks like to me,' she said.

'Then this will surprise you. This is from a spear, thousands of years old. I like to show it to folks who come to the base when they ask how long we have been here. Fifty years? No sir, I say. This has been a fighting base for a long long time. The Celts were here. You've heard of them? And the Romans. To provide responsive air combat power, to meet our allies' and our nation's international objectives.'

'The Romans said that?'

'That's our mission statement, ma'am.'

'So you see the Americans here as historically a continuation of the Celts and Romans?'

'Right on, ma'am. And if you don't mind me saying so, that's a pretty smart way of putting it.'

The bus moved slowly down what Helen presumed was the high street of Honeysucklelay. Joe pointed to a building which had a large sign, Honeysucklelay Middle School. 'We are pretty keen on keeping up with education. We have an elementary school and a high school as well. Would you like to have a look in to see how the kids are doing?'

Helen looked at Johnny. Johnny returned her glance. 'Perhaps later? After we have seen the responsive air combat power, eh Joe?'

'Sure,' Joe said.

He did not look sure, Helen thought. They should have looked at the schools, elementary, middle and high. Now he was unhappy.

'Tell me Joe,' Helen said pleasantly, 'do you do many of these tours?'

'Fact is, I don't ma'am. A few for visiting Americans. Brass, that sort of thing. Congressmen. Not for foreigners. Not since nine-eleven.'

'We are foreigners?' Johnny said.

'No offence meant, your grace.'

'So what can you show us?'

'Anything, as long as it is not off bounds. We have a nice little museum here.'

'Celts, arrowheads?'

'Some second world war stuff. Part of a Flying Fortress. You know this was a base back in the war?'

Joe looked hopefully at his charges.

'I'd love to see the museum,' Helen said.

'Right on, ma'am.'

The museum seemed a surprisingly long way away, although Helen suspected that Joe had taken a detour to kill time.

'Go right in,' he said. 'Feel free.'

Joe did not follow Helen and Johnny into the museum, which was unattended.

Helen said, 'Aren't you an MP?'

'I was. Now I have been put out to graze in the Lords.'

'I thought I recognised you.'

'I apologise.'

'Did I see you on the box? A demo about something?'

'No so loud. Subversive talk.'

'England's green and pleasant land. Something like that?'

'I didn't choose the title.'

'Is that why you are here?'

'All these questions.'

'Sorry. Call me nosey.'

'Well, nosey, can I ask you why you are here?'

Helen did not say she had been kidnapped and spent the night with a former dictator who had male problems. She might say that she was an undercover police officer on an investigation. That would account for her shades and the tarty lipstick, and would almost be true. Johnny seemed a likeable and intelligent man. She might need his help if Lucas tried to stop her from leaving. But perhaps not.

'Sorry,' she said. 'I was dreaming. I'm just a visitor looking round. Anything for a glimpse of those sexy Americans.'

Johnny smiled, but Helen sensed it was a smile of disbelief.

'It sounds easy,' he said.

'Oh you know Americans, always hospitable.'

'I'm the first parliamentarian to be allowed in for months.'

Helen stopped herself making a flip remark. It would have fallen on stony ground. 'But an RAF base?'

'Really for American Forces. RAF. It's a little joke we have.'

'We?'

'Those of us who want our bit of England back.'

'You guys all right?' Joe was at the door. 'Good news. I've spoken to my boss. The base is yours. Open house.'

Joe became a fount of information. The area of the base was so many hectares, or was it miles? It was big, anyway. Helen could see that. And flat. East Anglia was one of the great sanctuaries of wildlife. Towards the coast it gave protection to the bitterns, the terns and the oystercatchers. As you moved inland the fauna changed. At the base the birds were bigger, more predatory, their songs harsher and they belched fire.

'We have the most advanced precision guided munitions systems and a rapid targeting system, for near real time. We provide all-weather, day or night air superiority and air-to-ground precision capability and multi-staged programme avionics.'

This came not from Joe, at least not directly, but from a loudspeaker he had switched on which was located at the back of the bus.

'With the Eagle we have the world's premier air superiority fighter, capable of eliminating enemy air threats anywhere, anytime, providing an air combat capability never before seen in the history of air power.'

Some music followed. Joe turned down the volume and said, 'I should have played you this earlier. That was the end of the tape. I'm just rewinding, so you can hear the whole thing.'

'I think we get the message, Joe,' Johnny said. 'Helen?'

'I'm dying for a cup of coffee.'

Joe did not object. Perhaps he felt some relief that these two strange people had a taste for something ordinary. He turned the bus round. The landscape of the Eagles gave way to the homes of the falconers. The bus stopped outside a flat-roofed building.

'You are certainly in the right place for coffee,' Joe said

The interior reminded Helen of the canteen at the Yard. Perhaps canteens were the same throughout the world.

Joe produced three mugs of coffee on a tray.

'You won't get a better cup of coffee anywhere.'

Helen sipped her coffee and said, 'Starbucks. I'd know it anywhere.'

'You are a very knowledgeable lady, ma'am. When were you in the States?'

'Starbucks in London.'

'London, England?'

'Just round the corner from my flat.'

'Well, I have learnt something today, ma'am. You are sure it is the real Starbucks? Not some copy?'

'Sure as anything.'

'You know, ma'am, the more I learn about England the more amazing it sounds.'

'You must visit it sometime.'

'I mean to ma'am. For now America is good enough for me.'

Helen had prepared a polite laugh to acknowledge a humorous exchange. But Joe, she realised, was not making a pleasantry.

'You've never been outside the base. Joe?'

'Never left America, ma'am.'

The base did indeed make a competent effort to replicate America in a foreign land. But did Joe believe that it was a piece of sovereign American territory? Helen felt twinges of patriotism. Should she remind Joe that this was a part of England, that the Americans were guests there? She looked at Johnny, and received the tiniest, but emphatic, shake of the head.

Helen said she would walk back to the suite, but Joe said he would take her there. 'Important cargo, ma'am,' he said and sounded as though he meant it. Helen obediently got into the bus and was driven thirty yards down the road and allowed to get off.

'Thanks Joe,' she said. 'I hope you enjoy England, when you find it.'

'Sure will, ma'am. Take care.'

Johnny gave her a business card. Helen paused, then took out her own card from her purse. She looked at it: just her name and address and telephone number. What would Johnny expect? Personal services? Never mind. Life was loaded with disappointments. She handed over the card and Johnny put it in a pocket without looking at it.

Lucas had returned from wherever he had met the American political people. He was in ebullient mood.

'They are letting me have my Sulu back.'

'Just like that?'

'In principle. The details have to be worked out, but now I can plan. Are you happy for me?'

'Of course.'

'Say it.'

'I am happy for you.'

'Very happy?'

'You sound as though you are not too sure yourself.'

'Can I trust the Americans?'

Helen thought of Joe, superficially agreeable, but what? Even an American peasant could assume that everything, everywhere was theirs for the taking.'

'As long as you have something they need, I expect you can trust them. The way of the world.'

'I shall miss your wisdom, Helen.'

'All clear for me to go?'

'Foolishly I promised. But you have things to do. I make one request. Check on my apartment if you have a little time to spare. I will give you a key.'

'Mrs Lucas?'

'She has left England. She found it chilly.'

It seemed a brief valedictory, but Lucas did not offer any information about the wife that Helen had never seen and suspected did not exist.

'And do what you can for David Robinson,' Lucas said. I cannot help him from here.'

'David?'

'I thought you knew. Trying to blow up Nelson's monument. Stupid man.'

TWENTY-TWO

When Helen arrived back in London she went to see Carruthers Smith at the Foreign Office.

'A social call or official business?' he had asked over the telephone.

'A bit of information. Not official. About Sulu. To satisfy my curiosity.'

When Helen was seated in his office Carruthers said, 'I thought you had moved on from Sulu.'

'You are being polite, as always. Yes, I was dumped after the Americans complained.'

'But you still, as it were, take an interest?'

On her way to the Foreign Office Helen had deliberated over how much she would need to tell Carruthers about her recent adventures. He had to be told something.

'I still keep in occasional touch with Lucas,' she said. 'I know that he hopes to return to Sulu sometime. I was wondering if you could tell me briefly how things stand in Sulu. In confidence, of course. Just think of a novice copper wanting to keep up.'

'Sulu isn't really my territory, Helen. Never even been there.' A long pause. He fiddled with some papers on his desk. Presumably, Helen was thinking, he was wondering if she was worth a bit of extra effort. Eventually he said, 'You may be lucky. Someone we occasionally turn to for an appraisal on South-East Asia called in today to use our library. He may still be here. Excuse me for a few seconds. Help yourself to more coffee.'

A few minutes rather than a few seconds later Carruthers returned with his expert.

'Johnny,' he said, 'let me introduce you to Helen Berlin, a detective constable and soon, I am confident, to be a sergeant.'

'Hello, Helen. No shades today?'

'Detective's day off. I left my disguise at home.'

Helen was naturally surprised by the encounter, but not amazed. In her experience coincidences happened all the time.

'We have a mutual interest in English sovereignty, Carry,' Johnny said.

'Not much of a concern for the Foreign Office these days,' Carruthers said. 'What do you want? Shall I leave you two to plot our escape from Europe?'

Helen and Johnny exchanged glances.

'Will it take long?' Johnny said.

'A stroll in the park should do it,' Helen said.

Carruthers dismissed them with a wave. He seemed pleased to have his office back.

They found themselves on the path in St James's Park that Helen had taken on her first visit to Lucas at what seemed a long time ago. They chose a bench by the lake. The pelicans seemed peaceful today, or perhaps they had eaten all the pigeons they could manage.

'I thought I caught a glimpse of Lucas at the base,' Johnny said. 'But I wasn't sure. It seemed an odd place for him to be.'

'The Americans want to keep him safe.'

'I thought they were finished with him.'

'They want him back running Sulu.'

'That's what he told you?'

'He is pretty sure.'

'What do you think?'

'I know nothing of what is happening in Sulu. That's why I came to see Carruthers. He says he knows nothing either.'

'Interesting,' Johnny said.

'That Carruthers knows nothing?'

'What Lucas told you.'

'Is it true?'

'Could be.'

'But you seem surprised.'

'Nothing the Americans do is a surprise,' Johnny said. 'But it would be unusual for them to give Lucas a second chance. They are not kind to failure.'

'So he won't go back?'

'I am not saying that.'

'What about the new Sulu president?'

'Yes, that's the question.'

'Isn't she a nationalist? Sulu for the Sulans. Throw the Americans into the sea. Can we have our harbour back, please?'

'Is that what Lucas says?'

'I heard it somewhere. Perhaps Lucas. Perhaps I read an article.'

'It is a view being put about.'

'You don't believe it?'

A pelican was approaching a pigeon that was pecking at a chunk of bread that someone had thrown and appeared to be unaware of its likely fate. Helen stood and clapped her hands. The pigeon hopped a few yards from the pelican but did not fly away. The pelican stopped and the pigeon returned to the bread. Helen sat down without warning it again.

'Serve him right,' she said.

'Lucas?'

As Helen watched the deathly tableau by the lake she was in fact thinking of the other responsibility that had been suddenly thrust upon her. 'David Robinson.'

'The historian?'

'Sorry?'

'David Robinson. I wondered if you meant the historian.'
'Did I say that?'
'You said his name.'
'Sorry, Johnny. My mind's going. And so young too. Yes, he has written a book, if that makes him a historian.'
'Robinson on Gunnery?'
'Amazing. How well read you are, Johnny.'
'Flattery, flattery. It just happens that David needed some information about religious practices in the ships of the Georgian navy. The church's information office, ever helpful, put him on to me.'

Helen took several seconds to examine the conundrum.

'I suppose there is a connection,' she said.

'I am no longer a practising priest. But I was ordained, a long time ago.'

'I have to see him, I suppose. Could you come along?'

'When, now?'

'Can you manage it? I'd welcome a bit of support. Our last encounter did not end happily.'

'I'd like to see David again.'

'You may regret it. He is in trouble. Lucas told him to blow up Nelson's column to publicise his new book.'

'But hasn't succeeded, I take it, or no one has noticed yet?'

'He is technically incompetent, but everyone is now terrified of terror, even the incompetent sort.'

As they set off Helen took Johnny's arm. It was comforting to have God on your side.

They walked north towards the Mall. At Horse Guards Parade Johnny said, 'Could we pause for a moment?' He walked towards a doorway which had a notice by it, 'Cabinet War Rooms'.

'Isn't this where Churchill won the war?' Helen said.

Johnny bought two tickets. He looked solemn. 'This is holy ground,' he said.

He led the way down some stairs. Below ground there was a quiet church-like atmosphere. A recording was being played of one of Churchill's speeches. Helen watched two women visitors, in their seventies, she judged, so they would have been quite young during the war. As Churchill's syllables rolled out, a smile of remembrance came to the lips of one woman. The other woman was weeping. The power of words.

Helen turned to Johnny. When Churchill stopped speaking he closed his eyes and said something, but spoke so softly that Helen could not catch the words. A prayer presumably.

'Do you want to look around?' he said. 'No? Oh dear, I'm holding you up.'

'Perhaps Churchill needs preparation before entering his sanctum,' Helen said. 'I'll read a book first.'

It seemed to be the right thing to say. 'He deserves politeness, at least,' Johnny said. 'But for him we'd all be speaking German.'

Helen thought that an exaggeration, a wild one. But she did not have the scholarship to argue. Anyway, she approved of men with strong views. She took Johnny's arm again as they entered the Mall and walked through the Admiralty Arch and into Trafalgar Square where, as Johnny had predicted, Nelson was still holding out against the terrorists, and turned left to the Horatio Nelson Memorial Trust. David had said on the phone that he would be there most of the day, but not to leave it too late as he had to report to the police.

A notice on the door said 'Closed for Staff Holidays'. Helen reached for the bell but before she had a finger on the button the door had opened.

'Lucas not with you?' David Robinson said. 'Obviously not. Well, you had better come in. Johnny, how did they drag you into this mess?'

David did not seem to expect an answer, and Johnny made no response except to start to offer a handshake which was declined, or not noticed. David was already making his way into the interior. Helen followed him, past the reception area. Felicity, David's receptionist/mistress, was presumably on staff holiday or had been made redundant or even, Helen thought hopefully, might be helping the police with their inquiries.

They were now, all three, in David's office. Helen sat down. Johnny, after some hesitation, sat down too.

'I suppose you want some coffee?' David said.

To this rational remark there were murmurs of assent.

'It's only instant,' David said, against the rattle of cups in the corner of the room.

More rationality. Better and better.

'How's the new book going, David?' Johnny said.

David ignored the question. He said, 'I've been talking to Lettie about this mess.'

Lettie was David's dead wife. Helen knew of his post-mortem conversations with Lettie, so this was not new, although it remained unusual.

'How is Lettie?' Helen said.

'She wanted to talk about clothes again.'

Wanting to talk about clothes was a commonplace remark, quite rational. Of course, what made it extraordinary was that anyone in Heaven, if that was where Lettie was, should wish to discuss them. Helen glanced at Johnny. He knew David, although presumably he had never seen him in his post-Lettie mood. But he was a priest, or had been, so conversations with someone in Heaven would not be totally unfamiliar.

'Never mind the clothes,' David said. 'What about the eternities?'

What followed was an account by David of his conversation with Lettie. It went as follows.

Lettie: 'I can't talk about that.'
David: 'But why?'
'I can't say why.'
'Not even a hint?'

'I have given you one.'
'Say it again.'
'The mysteries'
'Not much of a clue.'
'It's not meant to be a clue. A clue might lead you to a solution, and then you would die.'
'And then I would be with you.'
'No more talk like this, David. I want to talk about clothes. I'm still wearing the things I died in.'

David suddenly shook himself. 'I'm sorry, Helen. And you, Johnny. Funny thing, religion.'

'I would not say yours was a religious experience,' Johnny said.

'Oh? Why do you say that?'

'I am an expert. Miracles are inexplicable, and they happen to people who are inexplicably chosen. Your experience is quite ordinary.'

'Talking to my dead wife, ordinary?'

'Talking to yourself. That's ordinary.'

'Did Joan of Arc have this difficulty convincing people when she heard voices, or St Theresa?'

'Don't mock, David. Be glad you are earthbound with a dismal little problem that will soon go away. The divine is nothing but trouble. Now let's have a bit of rationality. Helen wants to help you. So do I. What exactly have you been charged with?'

'Sorry,' David said with a meekness that surprised Helen. 'I was stopped in Trafalgar Square taking pictures of Nelson.'

'Is that all?' Helen said.

'Basically, yes.'

'It doesn't sound too subversive.'

'That's what I thought.'

'Were other people taking pictures?'

'Of course. Snapping away.'

'And that was all you were doing?'

Johnny interrupted: 'How many did you take?'

'A dozen rolls or so.'
'Around 300 pictures?'
'I suppose it would be.'
Johnny looked at Helen. Helen laughed, loudly.
'I don't see the joke,' David said.
'You should have been charged with gross extravagance,' Johnny said. 'How long was it before you were nabbed?'
'Half an hour, perhaps a bit longer.'
Helen was thinking about the disguise of innocence. 'I was just taking some snaps in Trafalgar Square and then I was arrested.' The police state. Human rights endangered. She should have been sharper.
Johnny was saying, 'So this chap was questioning you. Did he have identification?'
'He was in uniform. A policeman. Not at all a bad chap. Once I had explained that I was writing a book about Nelson he seemed very understanding. I took him back to the Memorial Trust to show I was on the level and made him a cup of tea. I suppose I talked too much.'
Helen tried to recall the theme of David's book. Nelson as a psychopath? Something like that. Controversial, but hardly likely to worry anyone other than a Nelson addict. But David had talked too much, that was what he was saying. In Helen's own experience of interrogation, limited though it was, one thing she had learned was to encourage talk from the person being questioned; perhaps simply by providing silence that demanded to be filled. The policeman had listened and felt that something was not quite right. The threat of a terrorist attack on London had done the rest.
'So they haven't locked you up?' Helen said.
'I had to make a statement at a police station and they said come back later. That's where I have to go today. I'm wondering if I should take a solicitor with me.'
'You are not on police bail?' Helen said.

'No, whatever that is.'

'Don't waste your money then. You won't be bothered again, unless you are caught putting a bomb under a Landseer lion.'

'What about damages? For wrongful arrest.'

'But you weren't arrested.'

'I had to go to the police station.'

'You went voluntarily?'

'Under pressure. The point is my life has been disrupted. I have had to close the Memorial Trust. I haven't been able to write a word. Felicity has walked out on me.'

Helen looked at Johnny, priest, politician, defender of the rights of the English.

'What do you think, Johnny, compensation for poor David?'

'About a farthing, I'd say. Unfortunately, there's nothing smaller. Nothing personal, David. You have had a little shock, and you are still upset over Lettie. But it's nothing, really. Nothing. I must go.' He got up and held out a hand to David who, to Helen's surprise, took it. 'I expect you're right, Johnny,' he said.

It was Helen's turn. How awkward farewells can be. She heard herself saying, 'I am sure Felicity will come back.'

As they walked away along the Mall, Helen said, 'I thought you were a bit hard on poor old David.'

'Not hard enough. He has no interest in religion. He said that when we first met. Fine. That puts him in the majority. But he heard a noise in the night and now wonders if it would be safer not to scoff. I find it difficult to listen to him. I am not a fortune teller looking into a crystal, or a quack you can empty your garbage into, and not have to pay. We have no language between us. He has no knowledge. It is as if I asked him why Nelson was attacking France and should I take my holiday there this year. He would be stupefied at my ignorance.'

'You are very hostile.'

'The church is having to get hostile. Being tolerant hasn't got us anywhere.'

'Vengeance is mine?'

'A new flood would certainly help.'

'Aids?'

'Only if people believed it was sent by a wrathful God. But nobody is turning to the priests. They are asking what is new in genetic engineering. We may have to wait for a nuclear war.'

'Why do we always assume that God is good?'

'Not all of us do. Heaven may not be constant. Perhaps political changes take place there. Muslims against Christians. It may now be a democracy, though it is difficult to imagine God being no more than a formal head of state.'

'God as a dictator?'

'That's how most people see God. They speak of him as they'd speak of all authority, respectfully to his face and cynically in private.'

'How did we get to be talking theology?'

'I apologise, Helen. How boring I am.'

Helen took Johnny's arm again. She felt happy, but she wasn't sure why. But nor did it matter.

TWENTY-THREE

Helen was in Lucas's apartment overlooking Green Park. She had been there for about half an hour and was thinking of leaving. She could tell Lucas that all seemed to be in order, if 'in order' meant that the place was empty and reasonably tidy. The crone who did his housekeeping had apparently left, or at least was out, and the kitchen was clean, with the dishes washed up. A park policeman said he still kept an eye on the premises and had nothing special to report. If only the rest of his beat were as quiet as this.

Helen was sitting on the sofa where on her first visit Lucas had shown her the book on Sulu before locking her in and putting a black pearl in her coat pocket. The book was still there on a low table, opened at a picture of the hospital Lucas said he had built. A picture and Lucas: an association of thoughts reminded Helen of Lucas's story of having his picture taken when he had won an election and was walking on air like Fred Astaire, and how he longed to have the picture. Helen had said that it would be easy to get a copy of the picture. Did that mean that she said she would? She was not sure if she had made a promise. She was wary about making promises. But in that bizarre setting at the air base, goodness knows what she had said. It would not be easy to get that ridiculous picture, taken years and years ago. Perhaps Lucas would have forgotten about it. Perhaps not. Helen remembered that he had said that he had adored that picture. You remembered things you adored. She supposed she might make some inquiries, so that she could say that she tried. Perhaps the Yard would have a copy. It had a big collection of pictures of suspicious people. But she would have to explain to the picture librarian why she wanted the picture. You could do nothing at the Yard without questions being asked. She picked up the phone and dialled Joel Butcher on his direct line.

'Yes?'

'Nine-nine-nine.'

'You want something?'

'You are all charm, Joel.'

'Sorry, Helen. Up to my eyes. What's up?'

'No hurry. It can wait. Give me a call sometime.'

'Now you are being awkward, Helen. Tell me what it is.'

'It can wait, honestly.'

A pause at the other end. Helen waited for the line to go dead or for Joel to plead to know more.

'I have said sorry.'

That was better. Perhaps Joel could be tamed.

'A chance to thank Lucas for making you a hero of Sulu. He desperately wants a photo that was taken of him years ago, when he won some election, legally.'

'Film?'

'I don't think so. A newspaper picture.'

'The British Museum has copies of all the newspapers ever printed.'

'Including the Sulu ones?'

'I dunno. Was it printed anywhere else?'

'Could be. Who knows?'

'Well, I suppose you can leave it with me. Do we have a date?'

'For the election?'

'For us, Helen.'

'Let me give you a call.'

She had tried, Helen thought as she replaced the phone. She could tell Lucas that she had tried, honestly.

As she lifted herself from the sofa her eye was caught by a stain on the carpet, a small pinkish stain, hardly a stain at all, noticeable only because the carpet was of a light colour. Helen thought that it was a shame that the carpet had been disfigured, however slightly.

She was pondering such presumed carelessness when there was a ping from somewhere. Someone at the door. Helen found the device that allowed Lucas to examine visitors before letting them in. A young woman's head came into focus. She should know that face. Of course, the nanny Lucas had found in the park. Alone, as far as Helen could see.

'You'd better come up.' She pressed a switch that released the front door.

'No little ones today?' Helen said when she opened the apartment's front door.

'I thought they might not be welcome.'

'Mr Lucas isn't here. They could have had a lovely time.'

'Can I wait?'

'You might have to wait a long time.'

'He asked me to call on him. About the job.'

The girl was wearing what might be described as job-seeking clothes. Not all that different from her nanny outfit, neat, reassuring, but slightly less formal. Helen tried to remember the girl's name. Cathy.

'Better sit down, Cathy. Tell me about the job.'

Cathy sat neatly and smoothed her skirt. After she had been talking for a few minutes it was clear that she believed Helen was interviewing her for whatever job Lucas had promised her. It was an understandable mistake. Lucas had given the impression that Inspector Helen, as he had called her, worked for him. Helen declined to interrupt her. She was curious to know what Lucas had told her. That information, though, was not immediately forthcoming. Cathy was in the process of explaining the tyranny of her present job. Her working day, it seemed, was an irregular

165

one. It was based, Helen judged, on feudal practices, its simple rule being that if there was work to be done, it should be done. The children granted her occasional leisure by going to sleep.

'But didn't you realise that when you took the job?'

'It was my first. I thought they were little darlings. The first time I saw them they were being read to, looking at the pictures and sucking their thumbs. Absolute darlings.'

'This was their mother reading to them?'

'Their mother is dead. Didn't I tell you? Probably killed by the kids. No, this was a temporary nanny, Australian. Backpacking through Europe.'

'Well, at least they liked books.'

'She drugged them.'

'Drugged the children?'

'It does happen. To survive. You've no idea, Helen. No one has who hasn't done the nanny thing. I love children's books. They are full of wit and wry wisdom. One I love has a letter from Goldilocks to the Three Bears, apologising for messing up their home. But the humour of it is incomprehensible to children. The best children's books are treasured by adults and guarded from children. I get the best success with a shopping catalogue. It has no wit or wisdom. It contains pictures of ordinary things. No fantasy. The children point to the pictures and I make up little stories about them... The stories are never finished. The children are on the floor. The shopping catalogue is being torn apart, a better way to pass the time than listening to a story. I am down on the floor with them. They climb on me. I throw them off. Determinedly they go into battle. Performance is what counts now. We are all wearing the indestructible overalls that pass as fashion. What did Victorian children do?'

When Helen said nothing, Cathy said, 'I know what you are thinking. Children are lovely. But they are lovely only to their mothers.'

'Well, so much for Mary Poppins. What job was Mr Lucas talking about?'

'I couldn't believe it. So much money. But then Sulu is different. It is foreign. You expect to be paid more.'

A memory came to Helen of an advertisement that Joel Butcher had shown her, offering impossible pay, that turned out to have been the work of Lucas. Something about being a security guard. Or was that a joke? Anyway, Cathy had been taken in by it. Probably there were others.

'Did Mr Lucas say what work you would do in Sulu?'

'Not precisely. He said I would be a member of his court. Is there something fishy about it? White slavery, that sort of thing. It is supposed to go on all the time in Asia.'

It would have been easy for Helen to give Cathy a short, sharp lecture about using her common sense when she was offered lots of money for apparently doing nothing. It might stop her being stupid the next time she was tempted. But Helen did not believe Lucas was in the vice business. He might be a murderer, but he did not seek to purloin young women. He was a collector of people. He had tried to collect Helen. He had once tried to collect her father. He had collected David Robinson, and had probably eyed Joel Butcher after giving him that idiotic medal. Goodness knows how many other people he had offered jobs to while he was in London, at great salaries; it reduced the risk of being refused. He had talked to Cathy about making her a member of his court. Quite medieval. There was something of the king about Lucas. She remembered Lucas telling her about his palace in Sulu. He said he liked to have people around him. It was his weakness, collecting loyal servants, and sometimes disloyal ones. Was it so bad? he asked. Surely no worse than collecting old paintings or old bottles? Helen had suggested they were useless people. Lucas had replied that it was a mistake to assume that only useful people were, well, useful. Think of them as furniture. Not all furniture was useful. Some was merely pretty, or beautiful. If you were a president you had all these big rooms to make seem a little less empty. Cathy was pretty, and could be beautiful, an enchantress of Sulu, the Circe of South-East Asia.

'Do you want to be a wotnot, Cathy?'

'A what?'

There must be only a few years between Helen and Cathy. Was she using a word already unknown to Cathy's generation?

'It is a fairly useless piece of furniture.'

Cathy still looked puzzled.

Helen said, 'I think that Mr Lucas is aiming to gather together some people to take back to Sulu, rather as explorers once brought back natives to show them off in England. That is what he meant by making you a part of his court. It wouldn't be a job at all, although you might be called an assistant or a special envoy or a comptroller or a private something or other. The European courts were always rather good at this sort of thing, as of course are the Americans now. But really you would be a wotnot.'

'Doing nothing?'

'Nothing.'

'It sounds lovely.'

'But the boredom?'

'I could do with some boredom.'

'You cannot read a book or watch television while being a wotnot. That would take away much of your value. Time goes slowly. You do not have the pressure of a proper job that makes time pass quickly. You have to make your own amusements in your mind, as people do when they sit as an artist's model, or are attendants at art galleries, or work in a champagne cellar, shaking bottles to prevent the sediment gathering, perhaps the world's most boring job. Mr Lucas presumably tries to compensate a little by paying bored people well, so at least they can pass the time thinking about what they can spend the money on.'

'My sort of job. Have I got it?'

What was Helen to say? Should she admit that she had played a little game with this foolish girl? Would, anyway, that be true? Lucas could add her to his collection and fly the whole bizarre ensemble to Sulu in a private jet to a gilded life of boredom, even the appalling Daugava. It was improbable, but Lucas was improbable. Yet he existed, had had a long and successful career under the patronage of the world's superpower, and believed that it was only a matter of time before it would be resumed.

'I will write to Mr Lucas and tell him what you have said. You must be patient. It will be good preparation for a life of boredom.'

'Can I see him?'

'He is not in London.

'Shall I give up my nanny job?'

'That would be inadvisable.'

'Back to the grind then?' Cathy looked at her watch. 'Cripes, they'll be getting into all kind of mischief.'

'Where are they?' Helen felt a tremor of anxiety.

But Cathy had her mobile phone out, and was dialling urgently.

'Yes? It's me. I'm most terribly sorry. Are they all right? Little blighters. I'm coming now. Five minutes at the most. I've said I'm sorry.'

Cathy pocketed her mobile. 'The fuss people make.'

'The children are where?'

'That's the point. Just over the way. The children's playground.'

Helen could not recall a children's playground in Green Park, but when Cathy started to explain how she had found it almost by accident, she interrupted, 'You'd better get along now. Your friend is obviously getting impatient. You should have brought the children with you.'

'I was going to, come what may. Then this woman said she'd be happy to look after them a bit, loved children. So I thought: fairy godmother.'

'You had never seen this woman before?'

'We exchanged mobile numbers. I could tell she was all right.'

Helen found nothing to say that would not be bad tempered. Cathy was at the door. 'You'll tell the president to get a move on, won't you? I'm getting desperate.'

Helen moved to the window and watched Cathy emerge from the house and hurry in the direction of wherever the children's playground was. She wondered if she should have arrested her for gross child neglect. She wondered if she should have gone with her to satisfy herself that the children were safe. In this state of uncertainly she waited by the window, and eventually, after ten minutes had elapsed, perhaps longer, she saw Cathy, now with a child on each hand. They stopped. One of children had seen a bird's nest that had apparently fallen from a tree. They pulled it apart. Nature does not build to last. They walked on. The children spotted Helen at the window, and a dispute seemed to have arisen. Presumably the children had suddenly become hungry with the thought of the large cakes that surely must now await them. Helen moved from the window and sat on the sofa. She half expected a ping on the bell, but even Cathy must have decided she might not be welcome.

Her mind turned to what she was doing before Cathy arrived. Nothing. She was planning to leave. Ah, the pink stain on the carpet.

She wondered if it had been made during Lucas's Liberation Day party. Someone careless might have dropped a drink, perhaps during the chaos when Butcher had thrown himself on Lucas's would-be assailant. Then something came together in Helen's mind. Nothing to do with the party. Something earlier. A gun. Helen got down on her knees. Close up, the stain was not pink. It was red. It was unlikely to have been made by wine. It had been produced by a thicker liquid which had solidified into tiny granules. Blood. Helen reached to the copy of the *Sulu Times* on the low table and tore off a page and fashioned it into a sort of container to hold the granules she scraped off the carpet. It would be analysed. Almost certainly it would be human blood, from the man in the body bag in the Thames. Something else for the Lucas dossier. She should have looked for it earlier. The carpet had yielded a bullet and now the blood stain. But it was only of academic importance. Whatever Lucas's fate, he was not to be arrested, charged and brought before a magistrate.

Helen went home, made some coffee and switched on her computer when the phone rang.

'I've dug out some stuff,' Joel Butcher said. 'Don't know if it's what you want.'

'Lucas looking like Fred Astaire?'

'Boris Karloff, perhaps.'

'Sorry?'

'Before your time. I always forget how young you are.'

'What exactly have you got, Joel?'

'A packet of photographs and some newsreel clips.'

'That's very good of you, Joel.'

'Good? Is that the best you can do?'

'Sorry. I'm really grateful. I really am.'

'Well, do you want to see them?'

'I do, of course. Let's fix a time. When would be best for you?'

'It has to be now. Here. At the studio. Otherwise they have to go back.'

Now was a little after seven in the evening. Not a particularly late time for people who lived an irregular day, like the police, TV people and double-glazing salesmen. But Helen had planned her evening. Was it really now or never? Helen was not sure now that she was desperately keen to see a lot of old pictures of Lucas. She had not expected Joel to get back so soon with his treasures, if at all. Perhaps he had suddenly fallen in love with her. How awkward.

'Helen. Are you there?'

'Lost in thought, old bean.'

'Do you want to see these damn pictures or not?'

A pause.

'I'm on my way. Remind me where you are.'

When Helen arrived at the studio, she saw that Joel had gone to some trouble to present the pictures in a helpful way. They were laid out on a trestle table in roughly historical sequence. A woman was fiddling with a projector. 'Mabel,' Joel said, 'this is Chief Inspector Berlin of the Yard.' Joel turned to Helen, 'Inspector, Mabel will run through the newsreel clips for you. But first I expect you want to view the pictures.'

'That would seem sensible,' said Inspector Berlin. She walked slowly along the line of photographs, occasionally stopping to examine one with particular care, and turning it over to read the caption on the back. She retraced her journey, then paused for a moment, apparently surveying the whole collection. She went to the middle of the table, selected one picture and put it aside, then, seemingly impulsively, went to the end of the table and selected another and put that aside too.

'Are there any more?'

Joel turned to Mabel. 'That was the lot?'

'All we have.'

'All we have, Helen,' Joel repeated. 'I thought we had done rather well.'

'You have. It was just a thought.'

'Something bothering you, Helen?'

A pause, then Helen said, 'No, nothing. Can I borrow these?'

Joel looked at the two pictures she had selected. 'I don't see the resemblance to Astaire,' he said.

'No.'

'Bit on the weighty side, old Lucas. Not the dancing type.'

'Perhaps not.'

'But you reckon they will please him? Remembrance of things past?'

'It is possible.'

'Or were you putting on a show, inspector? I was quite impressed.' Joel had lowered his voice, but Mabel was still fiddling with her projector.

'No, not a show. Genuine interest.'

'You're not just being polite? No, politeness isn't your thing. Are you holding something back, something I should know?'

'I am polite enough to say you have been jolly decent, Joel. I hadn't expected such a quick response, perhaps none at all.'

'Um, it wasn't entirely altruistic, decent Joel has to confess.'

'Ah.'

'I may do something on Lucas. You triggered some thoughts. All those eminent people who once freeloaded on Lucas. Interesting. Let's see the clips, okay?'

'Okay.'

'Mabel, when you are ready?'

The clips were quite short, samples really, edited from sequences as long as intestines. Mabel asked if the inspector wanted to see any of them in their context, but in fact Helen was hardly paying attention to what was on the screen. Her mind was occupied by the pictures on the trestle table.

'Well, what did you think?'

'Sorry?'

'Do you want to see them again?'

'No.'

'You look very thoughtful,' Joel said.

How irritating that remark was. She suppressed her irritation and said, 'So, can I have the two pictures?'

'No problem. Mabel will make copies. What about the clips?'

'The one with Reagan might amuse Lucas.'

'How about something to eat?'

Helen was hungry, but she was not sure she wanted a meal with Joel. She did not want to talk. She wanted to go away and think about the pictures.

'There's a pasta place nearby,' Joel said.

It would be churlish to refuse.

'A quicky, then. I have a report to write.'

As it turned out, Joel did all the talking, a monologue about the idiocy of his superior who had no appreciation of creative work.

'You've really been a help, Helen,' Joel said, placing a credit card on the bill. 'You really think I should?'

'I think you should. Definitely.'

'Even if it means walking out?'

'You have to make a judgment. Walking out? I don't know. Reserve your options.'

It was waffle, space filling. The pictures; that was what Helen was thinking about. But Joel seemed to think he was getting good value.

'You've been really helpful.'

'All part of the service,' Helen said. What nonsense people talk for most of the time.

Back in her flat Helen examined her package. The Reagan clip she put aside. It would be a little gift for Lucas. The two photos she had selected, she set side by side on her desk. She took a magnifying glass from a drawer and examined each picture with care.

Next day she took a train to Tunbridge Wells and a taxi to her parents' house.

TWENTY-FOUR

When Helen arrived her father was getting into his car. He got out again and they hugged.

'Where were you off to?' Helen said.

'Tunbridge. Bit of business. I'll get us something nice for supper.'

'I won't be here for supper. Another flying visit, Daddy.'

'I'll have to call you the Flying Squad.'

The Flying Squad. Her father sometimes seemed a hundred years old.

'How is Mummy?'

'Doing very well. Her Italian's coming along a treat.'

'But she is still in bed?'

'That is her life, Helen. You children, scolding your parents.'

Her father was getting back into his car.

'Will you be long, Daddy? I've something to ask you.'

'Can't you ask me now?'

'When you get back.'

'Important stuff? Secrets. Exciting.'

Helen offered a smile, but felt a touch rejected. Perhaps, she thought, she had expected her father to have got out of the car and usher her into the house. Now sit down. Is there something wrong? You look a little pale. You have been working too hard. You always did. A proper little swot you were. A worrier. Now tell me what the problem is. Important, you said. Well, if it is

175

important to you, it is important to me. You know your mother and I will do everything we can.'

Her father had driven away with a wave. Helen entered the house, a visitor to the nest but no longer a member of it. She went upstairs to her mother's room. As they kissed she felt the lure of a warm, used bed that had once been the comforting start of her day.

Her mother moved half a dozen books to make room for Helen to sit at the end of the bed. 'Now sit down dear and I want to know everything that you have been doing.' The words were conventionally welcoming, but to Helen they sounded like being given a penance for disturbing her mother's studies. 'But before you start pop down and ask Bessie to make some tea. I sometimes think she forgets I am here.'

There was no one in the kitchen. Helen boiled the kettle, made a pot of tea and carried it on a tray to her mother. She seemed to have resumed her studies and the books that she had cleared had been returned to their appointed places on the bed. Helen poured cups of tea for her mother and herself. The room, although well equipped for her mother's needs, with a television, recording equipment and bookshelves, did not have a chair. Helen squatted on the floor.

'Now what were we talking about, dear?' Her mother seemed to have forgotten her request for a catalogue of Helen's activities. 'Are you staying long?'

'Just today, Mummy. I have to ask Daddy something.'

'You've just missed him. He's gone into Tunbridge. His muscle pain is still giving him trouble.'

'The massage person?'

'That's it. I expect he told you. Daddy loves to talk about his aches and pains. And now, my darling I must rest, and perhaps listen to some music. You must come again very soon. Tell Bessie it was a lovely cup of tea. Just right. It wasn't but everyone longs for encouragement.'

Downstairs, Helen opened the packet containing the two photographs, looked at them briefly and returned them to the packet. There were doubts in her mind. What last night had seemed a notion, however wild, had become an absurdity, not just improbable but surely impossible. She was wondering if she should stay. She could call a taxi, catch a train and be back to her flat in two hours. She could leave a note for her father to say she had been called away suddenly. She had a telephone directory in her hands, looking up a taxi number, when her father returned.

'I thought I wouldn't go to Tunbridge. Not often I see my daughter. I thought you looked a bit worried.'

Darling Daddy, to forego his sex treat. True love.

Her father said, 'Too late for lunch, too early for supper. How about a sandwich?'

'Later, Daddy. I want you to look at something.'

'I thought there was something worrying you.'

'Bothering me a little. It may be nothing. Probably is nothing. I almost went back to London without saying anything. You'll probably laugh. But let's see.'

Helen again took the two photographs from the packet. 'I want you to look at these and tell me anything that occurs to you. Or nothing. Just say what comes into your head.'

Her father looked at the photographs for perhaps a minute, though to Helen it seemed much longer.

'Well, this,' he said eventually, holding up one of the pictures, 'is of Lucas at some kind of ceremony. The old rogue. He had a presence though.'

'And the other picture?'

'This picture? Well, again some kind of formal occasion?'

'And the person in it?'

'There you have me. Should I know him? Have I failed your test?'

'Let me be clear, Daddy. Do you not see a resemblance between the two men?

'A resemblance, of course. Two men, perhaps of similar age. Could they be at the same ceremony?'

'Have a look at the captions on the back.'

Her father turned the pictures over and pushed his spectacles close to his eyes. 'Yes, I see what you mean. They are both supposed to be Lucas. What a silly mistake.'

'And you think they are not the same man?'

'Think, Helen? Isn't it obvious?'

'In what way?'

Her father looked at the pictures again. 'You think they are the same man?'

'I'm not saying that,' Helen said.

'You are doubtful?'

'Yes.'

'Then have no doubts. If it is important, and I take it is, then take it from me these pictures are of different men. You want proof? I have the proof only of my eyes. What is it you look for in a face? If you love someone you look at the eyes. I have never lost a dentist's rather less romantic habit of looking at a person's teeth, the upper lip and the shape of the jaw. The mind did that for me, recognising it from when I saw Lucas all that time ago in London.' Her father picked up the other picture. 'Look here, Helen, you can see the jaw line is much weaker.'

'And one tooth appears to be missing.'

'Is that what put you on to this?'

'Yes.'

'Um, means nothing. A trick of the light, perhaps. Although the images are sharp. But a missing tooth can be replaced with a crown.'

'I just thought it odd. I'm pretty sure Lucas's teeth are all his own.'

Helen did not want to tell her father that she had been close enough to Lucas to observe his teeth, and in any case he dismissed this bit of detective work. 'They can match false teeth now so you wouldn't know the difference. But anyway you were on the right track. Now, are you going to tell me what this is all about?'

Her father, Helen supposed, was the one person she could confide in. Not Joel Butcher, not David Robinson, not Carruthers Smith, not her boss Jenkins, all untrustworthy in various ways, not the Americans. Certainly not the Americans.

'I hardly like to say it. Is Lucas, this Lucas, not Lucas at all? It seems impossible.'

'Ever read "The Count of Monte Cristo"?'

'Daddy! You are not being helpful.'

'Sorry. Great yarn, though. And based on fact.'

When Helen said nothing her father got up. 'Time for something to eat.'

He returned with a pile of sandwiches, meticulously cut. As Helen ate one she immediately felt hungry. Her father was good at sandwiches.

He said, 'So what are you going to do?'

'I'll have to check what I can. Have a look at the rest of the pictures Joel showed me, with the jaw line in mind.'

'And then? If it is true?'

'I'm not sure. What does it amount to? Perhaps just a surprising piece of history, that will eventually come out. Something for a future television producer. The Count of Monte Sulu. Perhaps you are right.'

Her father said nothing for a few moment, then, 'It will worry you until this business is over. Secret information is a dangerous possession.'

TWENTY-FIVE

Helen considered herself a methodical person. She was free of debt. She paced her working day. She made an effort to look after friendships. Until quite recently she had thought that there were at least two interesting men that she could depend on to provide escort duty for a young woman busy making a career in a difficult job.

David Robinson had nice table manners. Helen remembered with pleasure the extraordinary, and no doubt expensive, meal where she had enjoyed showing off with a sexy cigar. She had felt she could have been content living with David. He was tweedy, probably good at lighting fires, intellectual without being pretentious. But Lucas had shown him to be unreliable, a fantasist and probably an idiot.

Joel Butcher had a touch of glamour, showed bravery in tackling Lucas's would-be killer and would probably have protected her black pearl from being destroyed, or at least have bought her another one. He had helped her with the Lucas pictures. He was possibly an expert in bed, but she did not want to sleep with a man who would consider he was doing her a favour. Helen did not consider herself to be pretty. She took out her compact and looked in the mirror. Her face was what? Her father had once told her that every face, however imperturbable, was a catalogue of information, not all of it to do with teeth. He did not believe in the idea of a poker face. She had been impressed by the remark.

Like many of her father's remarks, it sounded as though it had been the result of a lifetime of thought.

But what information could she see in her face? Not much. Perhaps it only worked when you were looking at someone else's face. She reckoned she had a standard face, the bits in the right place and the proportions perfectly adequate. But not a pretty face. It was the sort of face for which advertisements for cosmetics were designed to make the owner feel inadequate. You need Brighteye to provide that extra sparkle that sets you apart from the crowd. Has your skin got that glow that survives the toil of the day? Helen sometimes thought she would like to be ugly. Being ugly was not the same as plain. It was easy to be plain. Most people were plain. Ugliness required originality, and cost money.

Francis Bacon was Helen's favourite painter, and Richard Rogers her favourite architect. She wanted to be near the Lloyds building when it fell down. It would be an ugly spectacular. She found the plays of Edward Bond ugly, but unfortunately they were also boring. Aeroplanes and missiles were boring without being ugly. They were plain. Ugliness did not happen by accident. It was contrived. Nor was it the result of neglect. Squalor was not ugly. A girl in white satin culottes with a grubby seat was merely dirty. Being in a squat was not ugly. Wearing cast-off clothes was not ugly. It meant not having any money.

Butcher had an ugly name, and his face was moderately ugly. But Helen suspected that Butcher's interest in her was primarily self-interest, the possibility of getting her to agree to appear in a television documentary; at least she was a contact at the Yard.

She had briefly wondered about Carruthers Smith when he had offered her a croissant after that absurd meeting at the American Embassy. One attraction of older men was that they were grateful. With half of their expected life over, they were content with small pleasures as they rushed on to oblivion like Einstein's trams. She was not revolted by the memory of the relief she had provided for Lucas. You knew where you were with father figures. But she had a perfectly good father, albeit one who had found sex in Tunbridge Wells.

She wondered if she should get another flat. Her studio flat was small. Helen had always lived in small rooms, at home, at college, even on holiday. Her parents liked small spaces. They said they were cosy. Their Kent home was very cosy. The studio room was not the smallest one in her life. It had a high ceiling, giving it a generous amount of air for its floor area. Even so, in Lucas's establishment it would do only as a fair-sized cupboard.

She realised that everything she had done over the past few weeks had had something to do with Lucas. Butcher, Robinson, Smith. Candidates for friendship, past and present. Now there was Johnny, former politician, former priest, authority on Sulu, an impressive record. She needed someone to talk to. It looked like only Johnny made it from the short list. She phoned him. He was waiting for her call.

'I was worried about you. Where are you calling from?'

She said was at her flat.

'Are you sleeping there?'

'Of course.'

'Do you have anywhere else you could move to for a bit? A friend's?'

'Are you trying to worry me?'

'It is a serious question.'

'There's my parents' place in Kent.'

'Anywhere else?'

There was Lucas's unused apartment. Perhaps not.

'My club. I sometimes stay there.'

'Don't say its name.'

'Why not?'

'Use your loaf, Helen.'

'You know its name?'

'I do.'

'You really think I should move?'

'Better if you pitched there for a bit. Is your flat secure?'
'Sorry?'
'Chubb locks on door on windows?'
'No.'
'Call yourself a police chief?'
'I've got nothing worth pinching.'
'You'd be surprised. Better check your papers. Anything about Lucas, bring with you or destroy. But don't hang about.'
'What's all this about?'
'I'll come to your club a bit later. You are not to worry.'
'I am worried already.'

TWENTY-SIX

When Helen got to her club her immediate worry was that she had not brought enough clothes with her. How long was she going to be barred from her flat? She should have pressed Johnny to be more specific. However, she supposed she could always buy some things to tide her over. She should not get diverted by superficial concerns. She had a swim, but did not wholly enjoy it. The business crowd had arrived at the end of their working day. She booked a table for dinner, and waited for Johnny in the bar, nursing a glass of orange juice. He had not said when he would come to the club, and Helen had assumed that he would have been there waiting for her when she arrived.

Now she was getting impatient, perhaps nervous. She blamed him for making her worry. She was on the point of going into the dining room and having dinner on her own when Johnny arrived, apologetic and looking a bit tired. He said he had been held up at the Lords.

'Some important bill?' Helen asked, and felt that there was a note of scepticism in her voice.

'More interesting than that. Picking up scraps.'

Helen offered a puzzled look.

Johnny said, 'Are you going to offer me a drink? Not orange juice, I think.'

A waiter was summoned and a whisky arrived. Johnny sipped it and said, 'Their lordships are good with scraps of information, rumours, scandals, tittle-tattle. It keeps them going.'

'Is this about me having to leave my flat?'

'In a way. You and Lucas.'

'I see,' Helen said. 'Or perhaps I don't.'

'A lot of their lordships know Lucas, or did. Many were ministers who benefited from his hospitality when he was in power. Fact-finding tours, that sort of thing, no expense spared. Some were on his payroll, bribed to say nice things about him. Remember, at one time he was one of the most powerful men in Asia. He wrote to some of them when he came to London. Some had the courtesy to see him. Some didn't.'

'Like the Queen?'

'At least she replied to his letter. Not everyone did that.'

'They didn't want to be implicated?'

Johnny sipped his whisky, then finished it and ordered another.

'A good reputation,' he said. 'Very important for politicians.'

'For anyone, I'd have thought.'

'Most people will be forgiven, a bit, for lapses. Think of the crooked businessmen who continue in business. People give a shrug of the shoulders: well, that's the way of business, isn't it? But a politician is finished if he is found out to be a transgressor. Take away his reputation and there is nothing left. Lucas in London has made them nervous.'

'Serve them right.'

'Their hope is the Americans will get rid of him.'

'Do they? I think I am getting lost. Aren't the Americans protecting him, their loyal servant?'

'I believe they want him out of the way.'

'Kill him?'

'It is best to be realistic. That is my guess. The Americans want him disposed of.'

'But why? Because a few dodgy politicians are worried about him?'

'I am not privy to the inner workings of the American mind, Helen. I am just reporting that Lucas is in a condemned cell.'

'To be killed, murdered, just like that?'

TWENTY-SEVEN

Johnny said, 'There are certain difficulties in a society that believes in the sanctity of the individual, the rule of law, that sort of thing. Lucas has been singularly unco-operative in getting himself murdered. The Americans believed they had devised the perfect plan. A gunman sent by Lucas's enemies in Sulu would kill him in his flat. Lucas's body would turn up in a body bag in the Thames. The new government in Sulu would be blamed. Newspapers would be briefed, with a few extra juicy confidential details to make the story especially interesting. Some regrets would be expressed, if only to cover the Americans' long support of him. He helped to keep the communists at bay. After a few days Lucas would be history. But Lucas, it seems, fought back. The would-be assassin was himself killed and, in charming twist, he was the one who left the flat in the body bag. The best laid schemes of mice and men. Good old Robbie Burns. The Americans were upset. They hate to look incompetent. They hated to lose one of their best agents in Sulu, but took comfort that at least he wasn't an American.'

'Someone took a shot at Lucas at his party. You know about that?'

'I heard about it.'

'Was that the Americans?'

'I'm not sure. Lucas does have ordinary enemies.'

'And being knocked over the Oxford Street?'

'Perhaps just Lucas being silly.'

General Ripley had taken it seriously, Helen thought. She told Johnny about the meeting at the American embassy, although he seemed to know about it already.

'Ripley does not like competition when it comes to killing people. You surprised him.'

'Is Ripley behind this?'

'He is taking orders.'

'So what is his plan?'

'I can't read minds, Helen. The best I can do is to make what I hope are reasonable deductions from known facts.'

'And?'

'Lucas is in Honeysucklelay. As things stand, he cannot just be killed. As you say, he is supposed to be under American protection. Before he can be destroyed physically, his reputation has to be destroyed.'

'Does he have a reputation?'

'Let's see. What do you think of him?'

'Personally?'

'No, you idiot. How is he seen generally?'

'He was a dictator.'

'A nasty?'

'I suppose dictators are.'

'A Hitler or Stalin?'

'Well, no'

'Why not?'

Helen saw what was in Johnny's mind.

'You have a point. There are degrees.'

'Most countries are ruled by dictators,' Johnny said, 'although they may not be called that. *Authoritarian rulers* is the usual euphemism. It is the way the world is run. They come and go. Those that are kicked out and manage to survive usually end up in the security of a democracy. The south of France is full of them. London has its share. The money they manage to take with them usually allows them to live unmolested.'

'Lucas?'

'Lucas,' Johnny echoed. 'But supposing they do something so unacceptable that they cannot be tolerated even in a forgiving democracy? Helen, who are the most feared people today?'

A random collection of frighteners came into Helen's mind.

'Sufferers from SARS?' she said.

'Not bad. I was thinking of suicide bombers, terrorists. Osama bin Laden, al-Qaeda, the destroyers of the New York towers. You can add SARS if you like. Perhaps Osama invented it in a cave in Afghanistan.'

'You think he did?'

'Come on, Helen.'

'But wasn't Lucas supposed to be a decent sort of dictator, who helped to keep Asia free of communism? Not a pal of Osama.'

'That's what everyone thought, wasn't it? But let's say the cunning and ruthless Lucas has turned out to have a grudge against the world. A bearer of malice, against democracy, against the free market, against globalisation, all that is good in life. He even feels hatred towards the Queen, just because she would not invite him to tea when he arrived in London. In what form did this resentment take shape in his twisted mind? He decided he would support the free world's enemies, the terrorists. His vast wealth, stolen from the people of Sulu, would be put at the disposal of Osama and his beastly fiends. Fortunately, the Americans found out the true nature of Lucas, just in time.'

'Would anyone believe it?'

'It is already turning up in the newspapers. The grave is being prepared.'

'But proof?'

'Leave proofs to Pythagoras. What proofs did the Americans offer about Iraq's links with al-Qaeda before they invaded the country?'

A waiter appeared to inquire politely if Miss Berlin still wanted her dining room reservation.

She no longer felt hungry.

'Shall we bother, Johnny?'

'Certainly we must. Routines are important in times of stress. It's what kept the empire going.'

'I didn't think of you as an imperialist, Johnny.'

'You can admire the stoicism of the empire builders without being an imperialist. I date the fall of the empire from the time the people running it stopped dressing for dinner. I saw a photo of Bush the other day without a tie. A bad sign, I thought.'

Later, seated at dinner, Helen was wondering whether she should tell Johnny that there were two Lucases, which in her mind she called Lucas ancient and Lucas modern. Her father had said that secret information was a dangerous possession. That sounded like spy stuff. Her father was a bit of a romantic. Monte Cristo and all that. The idea of two Lucases seemed dramatic when she had first tumbled to it, but surely it was no more than a bit of ancient history. Helen suddenly felt absurdly reassured. The restaurant represented order. The unmarked white tablecloth. A line of cutlery. She straightened a knife. Perfect. Johnny was right, despite his daft talk about empire builders. She chose the set menu without looking at it. She felt in good hands. Johnny told her a story about the Lord Chancellor and his fondness for Worcester sauce. Helen said one of her ambitions was to learn Latin. But quite soon the talk returned to Lucas. What was going to happen to him?

'Guantanamo Bay?' Johnny said. 'It is one option. The Americans can do what they like there.'

'Poor Lucas.'

'Don't get soppy, Helen. He's not worth it.'

'He's not a terrorist?'

'No, of course not.'

'Just an ordinary, everyday failed dictator?'

'That's about it.'

It did seem ridiculous, Helen thought, to shed a tear for one of the gauleiters of the world. Supposing she had never met Lucas, perhaps hardly heard of him: if she read of his disappearance, of his death, would she have cared? She tried to explain to herself why it mattered that he should not be killed. There was the rule of law. She was supposed to be an upholder of the law.

'Sentenced to death. Even the Soviets put on a show trial.'

'Come on, Helen. That's enough. You've got too involved. You have discovered that Lucas is a human being. I understand that. You are like the guard who befriended Hermann Goering after he was sentenced to be hanged at the Nuremberg trials and gave him a pill to kill himself. Was that right or wrong? As a failed priest myself, I don't know. If I have a view it is to live as best you can in the real world with all its injustices, otherwise you risk going mad. I am more worried about you than Lucas. You have got yourself in a nice little pickle.'

They were near the end of their meal. Helen could not recall exactly what she had eaten. The plates of food had been set before her and had been taken away when they were emptied. When the waiter had asked her if she had enjoyed the meal, she said it had been excellent, and no doubt it had. That was all

She divided the remains of the wine with Johnny. 'A pickle? Am I supposed to be running away from a pickle?'

'The Americans suspect you are in some kind of collaboration with Lucas. You stayed with him overnight at Honeysucklelay.'

'I was brought there by force,' Helen said. She told how she had been abducted by Daugava

'I suspected something of the sort,' Johnny said. 'But the Americans may not believe it. Now they are nailing Lucas for terrorism, anyone associated with him must be a terrorist too.'

'You mean they really believe Lucas is a terrorist?'

'At certain levels, yes. The people whose job it is to feed stuff to the press: they believe it, or at least they act as though they do.'

'What about Daugava? She is a pal of Lucas.'

'She works for the Americans. She is perpetually hard-up. I'll tell you a story about her. She was behind with her council tax for her flat. Bailiffs were threatening to sell her furniture. She asked Lucas to help her out. He gave her some money, but apparently not enough. Ripley heard about it and settled the council tax bill. Now he has her.'

'I'd better see Jenkins.'

'Jenkins?'

'I thought you knew everything. My boss at the Yard.'

'The Americans have told the Yard of their suspicions about you. I hope that the Yard people have confidence in you, but don't count on it. They hate political stuff.'

'Who do I trust, then? You, Johnny?'

'Trust no one but yourself.'

'I'm surprised at you, Johnny. A banality.'

Johnny smiled. 'Sometimes banalities are true. Another banality, I'm afraid.'

'I'm not sure I trust myself. What do I do then?'

'Something is niggling at you. Better tell me.'

A long pause, then Helen said, 'This may be something, or it may be nothing.' Another pause. 'Lucas, the man we call Lucas, is not the real Lucas. At some point he took over from the real Lucas.' She told Johnny of how she and her father had compared early and later pictures.

As Helen's story unfolded she watched Johnny's face for some expression of surprise, even astonishment. But he was a cool bastard. At the end of her account he simply said, 'Do you have the pictures?'

'I've carried them around ever since.' Helen reached into her handbag and handed the pictures to Johnny. He looked at them, quite briefly, took a little more time to read the captions on the back and returned them to Helen.'

'How old is your father?'

Helen told him.

'Compos mentis?'

'I think so.'

'In a court of law would he be convincing as an expert witness?'

'He convinced me.'

'All this dental stuff, the shape of the jaw?'

'Makes sense.'

'But you got Joel Butcher to show you all the pictures again. So you had doubts?'

'I double check things. I have this boring habit.'

Johnny said nothing for a few moments and Helen resisted asking for his opinion. Eventually he said, 'I want to think. A two-pipe problem, as Holmes might have said. Give me a few minutes. Order some more coffee.'

Johnny closed his eyes. Helen saw his lips moving and wondered if he was at prayer, making use of his old priestly connections, seeking advice from whoever was on duty in Heaven this evening. A waiter was hovering. Helen pointed to the coffee pot and the waiter nodded. Silence seemed to be catching.

Helen poured some fresh coffee and Johnny opened his eyes.

'There's none so blind as those that will not see,' he said.

'Are you being rude?'

'Perhaps to myself. Two Lucases. How bloody marvellous. How obvious. I should have guessed. It may be nothing, you said. I love you, Helen.'

'It doesn't sound very loving.'

'Let's see,' Johnny said. 'The pictures were taken in the 1970s, Lucas ancient in 1973, Lucas modern in 1975. Those dates mean anything to you, Helen?'

Nothing sprang into Helen's mind. She wasn't born then. But Johnny did not seem to expect an answer. He was asking questions of himself.

'South-East Asia,' he said. The Americans facing defeat in Vietnam. Sulu the Americans' most important supply base for its soldiers. President Lucas the staunch supporter of the Americans. What do you think, Helen?'

'All history to me. Wasn't there big opposition to the war among ordinary Americans?'

'And by the British. Harold Wilson was prime minister. A bit scorned now, but he kept Britain out of the Vietnam War. No, I told the Americans, not even a stretcher party.'

'You told?'

'Did I say that? A slip of the tongue. But that was Wilson's message.'

'You were working for Wilson?'

'I was. Yes, I was certainly working for him. But don't be too curious, Helen. All you need to know for the purposes of this story is that, yes, I was in Wilson's team. Yes, I had a trip to Vietnam. And yes, while I was there Lucas was on a visit too. I never met him, although we stayed at the same hotel in Saigon. He was given protection and he upset the Americans when he said he wanted to see something of the fighting. Some Sulu troops were involved in the campaign and Lucas wanted to tell his people back home that he had seen them in action in the jungle. That, anyway, was what reporters in Saigon were told.'

'It sounds reasonable.'

'Except that no Sulu soldiers were in Vietnam. The Americans had pleaded with Lucas to send some, just as they had pleaded with Wilson, and he had said no.'

'So why was Lucas there?'

'I don't know. I didn't think about it at the time. Lucas liked making overseas trips; most politicians do. He had visited most of the capitals of Asia. Perhaps the Americans made it worth his while. Just a quick visit, Lucas, and then we will see about Washington.'

'Let me be clear, Johnny. Did Lucas go into the jungle?'

'So it was said.'

'And then?'

'Back to Sulu.'

'End of story?'

'Not quite. Within a month Sulu troops started arriving in Vietnam.'

'A change of heart, or a change of leader?' Helen said. 'Do we jump to conclusions?'

'Never jump to anything. You never know what might be on the other side. But we might allow ourselves a cautious progress. Lucas did disappear for a few days. Reporters who asked to see him were told he was resting after his jungle jaunt. Eventually he was put on show at a press conference and he looked grim, grubby, unshaven, still in his army fatigues. His army minder said he had been on a tough operation. "Operation Lazarus?" said one waggish reporter.

'So they knew? You knew?'

'You heard this word Lazarus all the time. People came back from the fighting half dead but survived. Lazarus types. The reporter had a black sense of humour. The idea of a switch never arose. I may have been surprised by the sudden change of policy by Lucas, but nothing more.'

'You believe it now?'

'You must know, Helen, there is no such thing as certainty. But you come to a stage where you feel more certain than uncertain.'

'So the original Lucas was killed by the Americans in Vietnam because he would not send any troops to fight there, and he was substituted for the more pliant new Lucas. But where would they find him?'

'You ask very sensible questions, Helen, but you have to understand that in Vietnam at that time nothing sensible was happening. Apocalypse now. The film got it about right. I don't see a plan here. If I see anything it is a chapter of accidents. Lucas, ancient Lucas, killed. The Americans lost 50,000 men in Vietnam. If Lucas was foolhardy enough to go into the jungle he could have been killed, whatever protection he was given. Just another

Asian dead would have been lost in the statistics. But Lucas was a president; the head of a country that America hoped would send men to the slaughterhouse. So his death would not be disclosed until the American brass thought about how to limit the damage. Perhaps someone bright had the idea of sending someone back to Sulu in his place.'

'But who?'

'He had brothers. The Lucas family was known to be squabbling over the spoils of office. Creating a double is not that impossible. We now know that Rudolph Hess, Hitler's deputy, did not fly to Britain to talk peace. A double came instead and fooled everyone for the rest of the war. Saddam Hussein had many doubles and the sceptical Americans who found him checked his DNA before they announced their discovery to the world.'

'But can we be sure?'

'We can be sure that something odd went on during those few days in Vietnam that the Americans want to keep a secret. No wonder they want Lucas dead and telling no tales. It's not just their lordships who will be relieved when he is dead.'

'There must be others who know.'

'All the more reason to get rid of Lucas before some inquisitive journalist gets wind of it; perhaps has done already. Without Lucas to confirm it, the story becomes merely an improbable rumour, swiftly rubbished.'

'I must see Lucas. He is entitled to know what is going on.'

'Lucas must take his chance. You must look to your own safety, Helen. You are the unfortunate possessor of secret information.'

'So my father said. I reckon I can take care of myself.'

'That sounds like bragging, Helen. I am surprised at you.'

'So what should I do?'

'All I can offer is advice. You must use your own judgment whether to accept it.'

'And the advice is?'

'Go to see Ripley. Explain how you were brought to Honeysucklelay. He can check with Daugava. Be open with him. How you were pushed into this job of providing protection for Lucas, and how you want to say goodbye to the whole thing. He is an intelligent man, for a soldier. He can call off the hounds.'

'The hounds?'

'I'm afraid your flat has been trashed. Did you destroy anything to do with Lucas?'

'There wasn't much. But yes.'

'That will stand in your favour with Ripley.'

'Can I go back now and repair the damage?'

'I guess so. Better make a call to Ripley, ask when you can see him. Then get on with your life and career. Save all this for your memoirs.'

'I'll have to think about all this.'

'Don't think too long. Don't turn round suddenly, but three, no four, tables behind you there is someone who is almost certainly watching you. I noticed him the bar, and he followed us in.'

TWENTY-EIGHT

Helen did not own a car, and she felt a degree of superiority that she was contributing to the greenness of the world, purifying the environment and snubbing the oil barons, although, put simply, she felt that keeping a car in London was a personal encumbrance. For visits to her parents in Kent she would hire a car, one with the smallest engine available, usually a Fiat Panda. That was green, and it was also economical.

For her visit to Honeysucklelay she ordered a Panda, but when she got to the hirer's her eye caught a red Mercedes sports car. Well, why not? She needed some kind of pick-me-up for her visit to the base to see the loathsome General Ripley. Was the beautiful Merc available today? The attendant checked. Yes, it was. But it would not be cheap. The insurance alone would be criminal. Well, nor was she cheap. She handed over her credit card, the amazing invention that put off money problems until next month, or next year.

'Should I go over the controls with you, madam?' Helen stretched into the driving seat and felt the reassuring touch of leather. The voice of the attendant softened into a murmur. Helen had returned to childhood, sitting next to her father, whose love for sports cars was so ardent that he drove them to destruction. 'Is that all clear, madam?' Very clear. Helen started the engine. Perhaps she would never drive a Panda again.

On her way to Honeysucklelay she considered what to say to Ripley. Johnny had told her to be open with him. What did that mean? It sounded like a confession. But what had she to confess? True, she had strayed from her brief, continuing to see Lucas after Jenkins had given the protection job to the idiot Hobbs. But that was nothing to do with Ripley. She was not going to humble herself. She would behave with dignity, tell Ripley that she just wanted to clarify the situation and ask politely why her flat had been searched. She arrived at the gates of the base, prepared to be interrogated, finger-printed and probably strip-searched, but when she gave her name a guard waved her through, and courteously directed her to Ripley's office. The guard presumably rang through because Ripley was outside the office to greet her. He shook her hand warmly and, Helen thought, would have embraced her had she offered a cheek.

'It is really good to see you again, Helen. How was the drive down? You have chosen a good day. When I got up this morning and looked out, I thought, England at its best.'

Helen was momentarily thrown by the lyrical Ripley who had replaced the monolith she had previously seen.

'What a great car,' he said. 'You English coppers do yourself well.' Although Helen was still a novice in the art of interrogation, she knew at least that people had as many skins as a chameleon. She should not be surprised that Ripley had more than one skin. Perhaps he had an abnormal number. Which one represented the real Ripley? Perhaps none. Perhaps the real man only existed well below the surface, possibly known only to his wife, if there was one. Well, it was no concern of Helen's. She did not find Ripley interesting sexually. She felt no desire to probe into his mind. She should be pleased that today's skin was not the aggressive one. She would make her formal peace with Ripley and go home.

Ripley ushered her into his office. He said something into a telephone and a woman appeared with coffee.

'First, I have an apology to make. Your little flat. I won't go into the details. They would only bore you. I did not order your little flat to be searched. It was an error. Send me a bill for any damage, the cost of clearing up, and I will see that it is paid promptly, and generously.'

Helen felt a trace of irritation. Her 'little flat' was not that little. It had high ceilings. And what did Ripley mean by 'generously'? Well, don't get waylaid by detail.

She said, 'You had me followed?'

'You were followed. And I tell you why, Helen. We are interested in you.'

'We?'

'Yes, indeed. I will come to that.'

'I have to say, I am not used to being followed.'

Ripley laughed. 'I love the English. "I am not used to being followed." He tried to capture Helen's accent. A grim effort, Helen thought, but she smiled courteously.

'I will concede that I was not sure of you. Nothing personal. You did well at the ambassador's meeting I do not accord trust easily. But once I feel sure about a person, that's it. I am sure about you.'

How could he be sure? And if he was he was making a grave error of judgment, Helen thought. But presumably he was leading up to something.

Ripley said, 'Would you be interested in joining us?'

'The American army?'

'Obviously not. But you would share army values. What I am talking about is The Cause.'

'What course?' Helen said, absurdly.

'The Cause. Democracy, freedom, liberation, a better world, the things that America stands for. And England too, of course.'

What should she say? She said the obvious, 'I like the job I have, general.'

'Of could you do. We would want you to work hard at it. Jenkins says you are brilliant, and are destined for higher things. That makes us very interested in you.'

'What, as a kind of, well, an agent for you?'

Ripley chose not to answer directly.

'The Cause is more than a job,' he said. 'It involves a way of life. I have to borrow a word from our religious friends. It is a calling.'

'What exactly would I have to do?'

'Perhaps nothing. Or very little. You would do your job. That would be the main thing. Have the respect of your colleagues. A woman working in a man's world and doing it better than any man. But occasionally you might get an invitation from one of us. Perhaps we'd want an opinion about something. Perhaps there would be something on your mind that you wanted to discuss with us?'

'Is there anyone in the Yard in The Cause?'

'I have to tell you this, Helen, in the past we Americans haven't been too successful in finding out what is going on in the world. We have ambassadors, the CIA, all that, but, to put it bluntly, we have been too fixated with our own importance to bother too much about other views. We don't have a sense of what is really happening. Our intelligence people are not very good.'

'What would The Cause be, a kind of think-tank?'

'You could put it like that. Not bad, Helen'

'Like the Brookings?'

Ripley seemed surprised that Helen should be familiar with the group of right-wing academics in New York who tried to influence government policy. He probably thought all the English were peasants.

'You know the Brookings?'

'I attended one of their seminars in my last spell at college. I spent a year in America.'

'You are a constant surprise, Helen. Let me say this: The Cause would be happy to share the Brookings' view of the world. But we are not a public body.'

'A secret group?'

'That is our strength.'

'Sworn to secrecy?'

'A simple initiation. Nothing too frightening.'

It sounded frightening, like the Klan, or the John Birch Society, or those horrid Fraternity clubs at American colleges. Innocent words tarnished by their associations.

'Are others at the Yard in The Cause?'

'They might be.'

'But we would not know each other?'

'That depends in your level of seniority. Not at first, anyway. But you can be sure, Helen, that no disloyalty to your colleagues would be involved.'

Of course it would, Helen thought. A secret organisation in the police working for the Americans. Jenkins would have a fit if he knew. Unless, of course, he was in The Cause. He had told Ripley that Helen was brilliant. He had never said that to her, although he was pleased with her sergeant's exam result. He was the one who had decided she could be spared when the Foreign Office wanted help with Lucas. Was this a plot to dump her? She tried to rationalise. Ripley was a natural conspirator, even if he did not have a lean and hungry look. He was a bit on the tubby side. Sorry, Mr Shakespeare, but such men are dangerous too.'

'I can see you are thinking, Helen. I do not expect an answer now. This is all long-term stuff. Settle back into your job at the Yard, put all this Lucas stuff behind you, and we can talk again.'

'How is he?'

'How is he? Who knows?' Ripley leaned back in his swivel chair and looked at the ceiling, as though pondering what Johnny had called a two-pipe question. Men, Helen thought, seemed to regret the passing of the pipe. 'You know, Helen, I have an affection for old Lucas. A rogue, of course, but he was on our side against the commies. Reagan loved him. I have got to give him that. But what do you do about these old rascals, yesterday's men? If Lucas had been sensible he would have settled quietly in London, writing his memoirs, taking up needlework, whatever. But he had the crazy idea of returning to Sulu to a tickertape welcome. MacArthur was his hero. "I will return." Did you know that? The most popular thing America did in Sulu was getting rid of him. We are not too wild about the woman who has taken over. But at least she is popular, and so far hasn't been setting up Swiss bank accounts. Very worrying, you know Helen, money in the wrong hands. Money can turn into nasty things, car bombs, hijacks, suicide bombers, attacks on innocent Americans. You know what I mean?'

'I've heard rumours.' Johnny had told her that Lucas's name was being blackened. 'Do you think that Lucas is bankrolling the terrorists?'

It was, Helen supposed, a rash question to put to Ripley. Up to now, their meeting had been low key. Ripley had played the all-wise avuncular mentor to the innocent, but promising, English rookie. Now she was asking a question that suggested she wasn't quite so innocent. She might have knowledge. If Johnny was right, the Americans were after her too, whatever Ripley said about making her a comrade in The Cause. Perhaps the two were connected. Perhaps this was a trick to draw her out. Ripley was not to be underestimated. Perhaps, perhaps, perhaps. Well, so be it.

Ripley was in pipe thought again. 'Honestly, Helen, I can't believe that Lucas is knowingly supporting terrorism.' The metaphorical pipe was withdrawn. Ripley frowned as a man concerned with 'honesty' might be expected to frown when confronted with such an unpleasant thought, that Lucas might after all turn out to be a villain. The space was open for Helen to comment. She said nothing. She had said enough already.

'The question is,' Ripley said eventually, 'was Lucas being used? He was supporting a number of organisations for exiled Sulu people. Welfare stuff mainly. Was that money being properly managed? He seemed to have kept no proper accounts. The odd thing is that he seemed disinterested in money. We probably knew more about his bank accounts than he did.'

Again a pause. An invitation for Helen to contribute any information about Lucas's peculiar economy. She had to say something.

'I never could fathom Lucas's household,' she said. 'You know once he befriended a nanny and her two charges in Green Park and invited them in for tea, and what a big tea it was.'

Ripley grunted. Lucas's kindness towards hungry nannies did not greatly interest him. 'I am sure there are many sides to Lucas,' he said dismissively. The meeting was coming to an end. Courteously, Ripley invited her to stay for lunch, and courteously she declined. She asked if she could have a brief word with Lucas, just to reassure him that she had inspected his flat and that it was secure.

'You could if you knew where he was,' Ripley said. 'He left us yesterday.'

'He's gone?' Helen hated the sound of her voice, loaded with surprise. One reason why she had come to Honeysucklelay was to see Lucas.

'Yesterday, quite early.' A pause, then, 'No forwarding address.'

Ripley again waited for her to say something. He had changed his skin, or perhaps that was her imagination. She was imagining nasty things.

'You seem upset, Helen. I'm sorry.'

'A bit thrown,' Helen said, recovering. 'He left me the keys to his flat. I was going to return them.'

'I am sure he has another set...' A pause. 'Tell me, Helen,' another pause while Ripley put on his previous skin, 'did you get a bit close to Lucas? I don't mean in the physical sense, but, how shall I put it, emotionally?'

Of course he meant physically. The apartment at the base where she had spent the night was a goldfish bowl, probably with cameras in every corner.

'I was his minder. My duty was to give him whatever protection the Yard could provide. He was an awkward man in some ways.' Helen became aware that she was using the past tense. 'And no doubt still is. You really don't have a clue where he has gone?' Perhaps foolishly, Helen did not stop there, leaving Ripley to cope with a direct question and answer it with a straight lie. She went on, 'He thought he was a prisoner here.' Ripley chose to respond to this claim.

'Did you believe that?'

'It is what he told me.'

'Lucas came here of his own accord. He said he was unsure about his safety. We couldn't turn him away, although the RAF weren't too pleased. This is their base, as you will know. We were relieved when he said he was pushing off.'

Several lies there, Helen judged. Perhaps the only true bit was that the base was the RAF's, although that was misleading.

'Are you sure you won't stay for lunch?' Ripley said.

Helen again said no. She felt she had said enough already.

'I do have to be back in London urgently,' she said in a lie to round off the conversation.

TWENTY-NINE

When Helen arrived home she picked up the phone to call Johnny, then replaced it. She remembered Johnny's warning: it might be bugged. She thought it probably wasn't: a police tutorial she had once attended said bugging was costly and should be used sparingly, certainly not for unimportant people. She was certainly not important. She picked up the phone again, and again put it down. Supposing the Americans had put a tap on her phone? They had plenty of money. She could, she supposed, go to the Yard and make any calls from there, unobserved except by a dozen nosy people in the crowded room where she had a desk. She could send Johnny an email or a snail mail, or send him a message by pigeon. She picked up the phone again. What did it matter if the Americans did know of her conversation? It was clear that nothing she would say to Johnny would be a surprise to Ripley.

'Yes?' Johnny's voice, only the cultured accent identifying the owner.

A new thought came to Helen. Could she trust Johnny? She was in a state today.

'Is he dead?'

'Calm down, Helen.'

'I don't feel calm.'

'Don't say anything more. I'll come round.'

The line went silent. Helen tried to calculate how long it would take Johnny to make the journey. He lived in Southwark, a district south of the Thames. If the tube was working properly, always a possible hazard, he might get to Helen's West End flat in half an hour, well, say three-quarters. He arrived in twenty minutes.

'I was lucky,' he said. 'I got a taxi.'

'I do appreciate this, Johnny. But I'd have talked on the phone.'

'Better not for me. You have the whole of the Metropolitan Police to protect you, Helen.'

'Are you so worried, Johnny?'

'Don't let's go into that. Did you make your peace with Ripley?'

'He was suspiciously agreeable.'

'He doesn't want to make more enemies than he needs to. You are a possible ally in the future; at least that is what he thinks.'

Helen wondered whether to tell Johnny about The Cause. She decided not to, although she wasn't sure why.

'Lucas has left the base.'

'So I gather from your shout over the phone. No forwarding address?'

How odd, Helen thought, those were the words Ripley had used.

'Oblivion cemetery, second gravestone on the right?'

'Possibly,' Johnny said. 'But perhaps not probably.'

'Your reasoning for that?'

'More a feeling. If Lucas had been done away with, surely it would be public knowledge by now. In the papers, something at the end of television news. A car accident, a terrorist attack, whatever. Finito. The end of Lucas. The Americans wouldn't want a mystery, with the idea growing that he was still alive, that one day he would return to Sulu. They still believe in ghosts in Sulu.'

'So where is he? Is he still locked up in Honeysucklelay?'

'He may have just left, as Ripley told you. Not everything he says is a lie.'

'I am confused.'

'A normal condition of the world.'
'So what am I to do?'
'What was Ripley's advice?'
'Forget Lucas. Get back to my job.'
'I can't better that.'
'What, give in?'
'That's childish talk, Helen.'

Helen felt she should be offended, but was not. Children were usually sensible, applying simple logic to problems that baffled grown-ups. It was adultish talk that sickened Helen. Lucas might be a rogue, possibly a murderer, but he was entitled to be protected from Ripley's lynch law. A childish idea had come into Helen's mind. She would arrange for a warrant to be issued for Lucas's arrest, on a suspicion of murder. It should not be difficult. The warrant would need a magistrate's authorisation. But that would be a formality. As a police officer she would provide the necessary evidence to back the warrant. All police forces would be circulated with Lucas's description. There would be stories in the newspapers. If Lucas was still alive he would be found and kept safe in a police cell.

'Don't do anything daft, Helen.'

Helen said nothing. She considered the daftness of her notion. As soon as Jenkins heard of it he would cancel the warrant. She would be on a disciplinary charge, probably suspended, perhaps sacked. She would have made a gesture, but would it be a pointless one? She did not want to be a plaster heroine, as ridiculous as the role Lucas had given her as a rebel fighting for the communists in Sulu. Lucas: he did have a hold on her. She did not know why. Or perhaps, somewhere in the chambers of the mind that are best kept locked, she did.

Johnny said, 'Is this Ripley's work, or the normal state of things?' His hands made a circuit of the room.

Helen had done her best to restore the flat, but had achieved only a rough tidiness.

'Ripley said it was a mistake, and I would be compensated, generously. Trying to bribe a police officer. Ten years for that.'

'You must have impressed him. No one has offered me anything.'

'You've been done over?'

'Several times. Once by your people. Twice by the Americans. Once by the Russians, or it may be been the Ukrainians.'

'No wonder you're careful.'

'Not careful enough. My new strategy is to put a notice on the door, saying everything is unlocked, there is nothing worth taking and not to break anything. On the other hand, it seems unfair that the hoodlums should go away empty handed. They have a living to make. So I usually leave something interesting, a map of the Pennines heavily annotated, a picture of George Bush with kind greetings to me and a smudged photocopy of a Vietnamese restaurant menu.'

Johnny spoke casually, but he did not smile. He was under strain.

'I do appreciate you helping me,' Helen said.

'You must understand I can do little except to try to persuade you not to be an idiot. These are deep and treacherous waters, Helen. Swim away while you can.'

Johnny's mobile phone rang some cheerful air that only made him frown.

'Yes? Yes. I see. Yes. Thank you.'

He switched off the phone and placed it with its unwelcome contents in his pocket.

'The hoodlums have struck again. I'd better go. Better not call me unless you have to. But don't hesitate if you need a shoulder.' She stood to give him a farewell peck and they fell into a sexless embrace. 'Take care.' 'Take care?' Banalities should not be despised, Johnny had said.

When he had gone Helen dialled her telephone call-minder. The Roedean voice said she had three saved massages and one new message. The new message was brief and puzzling. A male voice said, 'Lucas expects.' That was all. Helen listened to it again and stored it. She made a cup of coffee and listened to it once more. It declined to give up its secret. If it was a coded message it meant no more to her than the Morse code. The caller was presumably being careful, believing that her phone was bugged. But so careful that she had no idea what it meant. How irritating.

She called directory inquiries and explained that she wanted the number of a caller who had left a message. The operator gave her a number to call, but it turned out to be Roedean voice, who said she had four saved messages and no new messages. Helen hung up. Somewhere among the infinite machinery of British Telecommunications there would be the number she wanted. Perhaps by applying endless patience, speaking to numerous people in the company's call centres in India and Vietnam, it would, before she was too old to care, be revealed to her. There must be an easier way.

Lucas. That was clear enough. The decoding experts who had won the war from Bletchley Park would have been grateful for such a clue. But *expects*? Lucas expected something from Helen. But what, and where and how? The problem remained with Helen all day. It was only after she went to sleep that the brain was able to consider the problem quietly, undistracted by Helen's other random worries, and offer an elegant solution that was clearly correct.

She awoke at seven impressed by her cleverness, and impatient to put the solution to the test. She showered, had coffee and toast for breakfast and set out on her mission. The West End was filling up for the day's duties, the shops and offices opening, the traffic starting to thicken. Portland Place smelt fresh from its morning wash. Oxford Circus was already dirty. In Regent Street a smashed window was being boarded up. And so to Trafalgar Square; turn right to the offices of the Nelson Trust. The admiral expected. So, it seemed, did Lucas.

The front door of the trust was closed. A notice on the door said the curator was away, but gave a number to call for emergencies. The now code-minded Helen wondered if this was a message for her, but decided to use the more time-tested method of banging on the door. A curtain moved at a window on the second floor. A minute later the door was opened by David Robinson. 'Quick, don't hang about,' he said.

Helen stood for a moment on the threshold, but Robinson took her arm and hustled her in and bolted the door against the problems of the world. She followed him upstairs to the flat where not long ago he had cosily installed himself. A sofa had been made up into what looked like a not too comfortable bed. Lucas had presumably taken over the bedroom.

'Is he still in bed?'

'I suppose so, or hiding. God, what a mess.'

A number of adjectives came into Helen's mind as she contemplated Robinson, now sitting on his rumpled bed-sofa. 'Dejected' about summed him up. He was no longer the Robinson whose life had seemed rather well controlled; the historian who had published a small but well received book; the suitor who had charmed her over a delicious meal; even the widower who had seemed to be taking his bereavement exceptionally well. Helen wondered what had become of Felicity, Robinson's new soul-mate. Better not to ask.

'Why did he come here?' Robinson said.

'Nowhere else to go, I suppose.'

'Hotels, that posh flat.'

Helen did not answer. The answer was obvious.

'What did he tell you?' Helen said.

'Not much. He just arrived and said he wanted to stay here a bit. Gave me that silly message to give to you. Told me to change my voice a bit. I tell you, Helen, I'm a bit worried.'

'I dare say Lucas is worried too.'

'You are not being much help.'

211

Helen was not in a helpful mood. Lucas was calling in a debt. Robinson should understand that. No free dinners.

'Brace up, David. But for Lucas you wouldn't be here at all.'

'I did all the work. All he did was to give me a few contacts. I wish I had never met him. A bad lot. All that business about blowing up Nelson's statue. Crazy. Is he running away from something?'

'He must be pretty desperate to come to you.'

'And why are you here? That's what I don't understand.'

One of the many things beyond Robinson's understanding, Helen thought. She gave him a formal answer, all that he deserved.

'Lucas is a guest of the British government. As such he is entitled to protection. I am part of that protection.'

'But all this coded stuff?'

'Lucas has enemies. Secrecy is part of the protection.'

'So are you going to take him away? Put him a police station?'

Helen almost smiled. That wasn't far from her notion of issuing a warrant for his arrest. She supposed she would take him away if he had nowhere to go. She wondered if he could stay with her parents in Kent for a time. Her father, anyway, would be thrilled, and her mother was locked into her own fantasy life.

'It is possible. I will have to see what Lucas says.'

'That makes me feel a lot better.'

It would, Helen thought. Shit.

The bedroom door opened. Lucas, former president, former defender of western values, former ally of America, made his entrance.

THIRTY

What slightly surprised Helen was how composed Lucas seemed. The image that came into her mind was of a dish that had turned out perfectly even though the kitchen was rudimentary. Lucas had shaved carefully and had presumably showered: his hair was still damp. He was wearing a well-cut grey flannel suit with a green knitted tie. His shirt had been well pressed. In the buttonhole of his jacket was a tiny enamelled pin, which Helen recognised as the Sulu flag. Nothing flash. The former president was conveying discretion.

'Well,' he said, 'are we ready?'

Ready for what? Helen turned to Robinson, who looked blank.

'Breakfast,' Lucas said. 'The famous English breakfast.'

'I'll put the kettle on,' Robinson said.

Lucas seemed not to have heard. He looked at his watch. 'We must go. I like to be prompt.' He moved though the room and went downstairs to the front door. Helen and Robinson followed him. By the time they were outside, Lucas had hailed a taxi.

'We could walk,' he said. 'It's not far. But when a London taxi offers itself you should take it. It is a good sign at the start of the day.'

The taxi headed in the direction of St James's Palace, turned right into St James's Street, then left into St James's Place and stopped outside a pleasant building that a brass plate disclosed was the Royal Over-Seas League.

'Your club?' Helen said.

'I have an honorary membership from happier days. It is a friendly place. Royal. Slightly old-fashioned. Over the seas. You know what they mean. Better than Brooks or the Athenaeum for our needs, I thought.'

Helen did not disagree. She had no knowledge of either Brooks or the Athenaeum.

Lucas was by now at the club doors. Robinson was fumbling for money to pay the taxi driver. Helen paused for the transaction to be competed, then followed Lucas into the club.

Lucas spoke to a receptionist, then led the way to the dining room. 'All is ready,' he announced.

A table had been set for five people. As Lucas, Robinson and Helen sat down, two waiters approached with trays of fried eggs, bacon and kedgeree and set them among toast, croissants, jams, a pot of coffee and a teapot of tea.

'Is there anything else, sir?'

Lucas looked inquiringly towards Helen and Robinson.

'I am sure it will do for a start,' Helen said. The breakfast was, she thought, a suitable partner for the famous English teas that Lucas had provided. She wondered what Lucas would provide for the famous English lunch.

'We must save something for our other guests,' Lucas said. 'But I do believe…yes.' He was on his feet and greeting Joel Butcher and Cathy the escapee nanny.

'So good of you to come,' he said.

Joel lifted a video camera from his shoulder and set it on the floor beside his chair.

'Heavy beast,' he said, 'but I thought I'd better cart it along. Now what's the set-up here?' He looked around the table, as though noticing its occupants for the first time. 'Helen! And David! This all looks very conspiratorial.'

Lucas said, 'Now tuck in. I do not eat a large breakfast myself. It is not an English habit I have yet acquired, and as I will be leaving the country soon it is an accomplishment that I will have to postpone for another day. All of you here have in your own way contributed to my pleasure in England. With David, a gifted historian with a great future, I have had many hours of intellectual talk, opening my eyes to entirely new aspects of England's naval story. When I found myself a little tired and looking for a refuge, he willingly threw open his home to me, insisting even that I have his bed. Joel Butcher, we all know, is the most brilliant of the new generation of television innovators, and a brave man, the recipient of Sulu's highest award for valour for his action in saving my life. And little Cathy here, caring, thoughtful, representing the best and the brightest of those who have made their careers in improving the lot of the deprived. And what can I say about Helen Berlin, the jewel of the British police force, who has given me round the clock protection regardless of her own comfort and safety?'

The heroes of breakfast table, Helen observed, were greedily accepting their rewards. She had fancied some kedgeree, but the dish was now empty. She took an egg and some bacon and put aside a croissant for later. None of the heroes seemed to have objected to Lucas's fantastic account of their achievements. Flattery is the lie that is always believed. The one bit of truth that Lucas had uttered was, presumably, that he was leaving.

Lucas had taken a piece of toast and was carefully anointing it with a scrap of butter. 'I won't tell you where I am going, not at this moment. Those that choose to come with me will of course be told well in advance. For now, let me say, the place of destination, indeed destiny, is safe and interesting. Joel would have creative opportunities previously unimagined even to his fertile mind. I see the Palm d'Or beckoning at Cannes. The place would provide David with the material for what I believe would be his masterwork. And little Cathy would find her caring world infinitely expanded.' Lucas seemed to be undecided whether to add marmalade to his toast. He had drawn the marmalade dish towards him, but then pushed it away as an unnecessary extravagance.

'You would not be committing yourself for a lifetime,' he said. 'You could even think of it as a holiday, with all expenses paid. I ask for nothing in return except your companionship.' Lucas finished his piece of toast and presumably his breakfast. 'I would welcome any thoughts.'

Cathy said she would like to come, but would have to ask her mother. She was blessed with a smile from Lucas. Joel said that he had a lot of work in hand. He could not give an immediate decision. He would anyway need to know more. But he liked the idea of a foreign project. He had to push off now, but he would keep in touch. Thanks for breakfast. Then, with his camera on his shoulder, he had gone. David said that it was a big decision, 'a very big decision'. He wiped his lips with a napkin and said he had better be off to open the shop. Cathy asked where the loo was and when she returned said she had no money to get home; the taxi to the club had cleaned her out, and weren't taxis expensive? Helen gave her a ten-pound note.

Helen found a pot of coffee in the wreckage of the table and held it aloft. Lucas nodded and she filled his cup and her own.

'Well, at least Cathy gave you a firm answer,' she said.

'They will all come,' Lucas said. 'And perhaps others. You are the only one I am not sure about.'

'You can be sure. The jewel of the British police force is quite certain.'

'I am not used to no.'

Helen shrugged. 'Nothing personal. I have a career to master. It does not include exotic holidays of indeterminate length. Where are you taking them anyway?'

'To Russia, then to Vietnam.'

Helen knew nothing of either place, except what she had read in the tourist sections of the weekend papers. In the world that had succeeded the cold war both countries were regarded as friendly, even benign, immune seemingly even from suicide bombers. Still, Lucas would be leaving the protection of mother Europe. If he no longer cared for Britain, there was France. Plenty of former dictators lived in France.

'Do you have to go?'

'Come on, Helen. Use your mind. You know I am a hunted man. I cannot even go to my apartment. I am having to use David Robinson's disgusting premises.'

'I am confused.'

'You are not confused, Helen. You are playing at being confused. The man you know as Johnny has told you that the Americans are after me.'

Now Helen was confused. 'I know as Johnny?'

'He has, I believe, several names.'

'And you are his friend?'

'We know each other. He helped me to get out of Honeysucklelay.'

'I was there yesterday. You know that?'

'Of course.'

'Ripley said that you had left.'

'Did you believe him?'

Helen tried to recall exactly what Ripley had told her.

'He said that you had come to the base for protection, but had decided to leave. He had no idea where you were.'

'I was, I suppose, lured to the base. It was a stupid thing to do. But the Americans were cunning, unusually cunning for Americans. They said they wanted to discuss my return to Sulu. Not, they explained in their unusually cunning way, as president, that would not be possible at present, but as a member of the government. How could I resist? I am an addict for Sulu. Sulu is my heroin.'

'Ripley was your dealer?'

Lucas smiled bleakly at the play on words.

'Ripley is rich,' he said. 'For now.'

Helen paused at the seeming non-sequitur. Then she said, 'You gave him money?'

'Yes.'

'He held you as a hostage for money?'

'You should arrest him, Helen. Put him in the Old Balliol.'

'Bailey. Old Bailey.'

'Tyburn. Hang, draw and quarter. To the Tower. The Traitor's Gate.'

Lucas's flight of fancy was uttered with bitterness.

A fresh pot of coffee had arrived on the table. Helen refilled Lucas's cup. She wanted to ask him how he had paid Ripley. Did he carry around with him a trunk full of cash, in easily manageable denominations, to buy himself out of difficulty situations? Or did he simply write a cheque? There's a million pounds, Ripley. Now can I go? She had been waiting for Lucas to ask about the picture of him looking like Astaire, and had a simple answer ready: that she had not been able to find it. Johnny had advised her not to tell Lucas she knew of his past. Know-alls can get hurt, he said; her father's view, too. Not all men were stupid. But no request for a photo had been made. It was hardly high on the list of preoccupations of a man threatened with death.

She said, 'So where is the general now?'

'Now exactly? He should have reached New York by now. It depends on the flights. But he will certainly be in Cayman pretty soon.'

Helen sought to decipher what Lucas was saying. Why could he not be clear? Cayman was presumably the Cayman Islands, a British colony in the Caribbean, noted for its banks that did not ask too many questions. Ripley, Lucas seemed to saying, would be on his way there to collect his hostage money. Helen thought of the two men discussing matters of life and death in Ripley's office at Honeysucklelay, or perhaps in Lucas's apartment for more privacy. Would they have raised their voices? The issues were too serious for that. How much would Lucas pay to escape the trap that Ripley had prepared for him? Ripley might start by asking for the lot, every dollar in Lucas's fortune. That would be a cheap price to pay for your life, he would say. A short auction of death would follow and a sum would be agreed. After doing whatever deal he had done with Lucas, Ripley would have got on a flight from Honeysucklelay to America, to another military base there, and then taken a domestic flight to New York, and was now waiting for a connection to the Caribbean. Lucas would not only have bought his freedom, but he would have also bought some time.

'So you are safe for a bit?'

'Safe, Helen? Not very safe. Ripley may have accomplices. They may be waiting outside poor David Robinson's place at this very moment. I hope they are not. I believe Ripley is normally greedy and has no wish to share his new wealth with others. So he is acting on his own, will collect his money, and return to Britain in a few days. But I am guessing, and taking what precautions I can.'

'But surely it is not just Ripley. From what Johnny says, it is the American government that wants to do you in.'

'That is very dramatic, Helen. I do not think President Bush will have ordered my murder. It is unlikely that he will have even heard of Sulu and its problems; geopolitics is not one of his strengths. Decisions about getting rid of unwanted former allies are taken at a much lower level. Who is Ripley? He is a general of middling rank, but what else is he? Does he wear other uniforms, or no uniform at all?'

Helen was not sure she should be listening to all this. Every so often during the Lucas affair she would suddenly remind herself that she was a police officer bound by simple rules designed to protect her and the service. Two of the most important rules involved The Notebook and The Statement. *I can find no entry at all in your notebook for the past month, Constable Berlin. And when Mr Lucas told you that he feared for his life, why did you not take a statement from him? You must realise that such a document would be of great value now that we are trying to find his killer.*

A waiter was hovering. Would it be convenient to clear the table? Lucas nodded. 'I like meals,' he said. 'They are an interlude between problems.'

Helen said, 'Are you going back to David's place?'

'Do you think I should?'

'Not if you feel unsafe there.'

'I seem to have a choice between places that are unsafe and very unsafe.'

'I was wondering about my parents' home in Kent. They'd put you up for a bit and you could reminisce with my dad about the job you offered him.'

Lucas said nothing for a few seconds, then, 'You are extraordinarily kind, Helen. But I will remain in London. There are arrangements to make. I will stay here, at the club, with all the others from overseas. Everyone is very friendly. The club is for members only. Assassins are not admitted.'

Helen laughed. A joke in the present circumstances deserved to be rewarded.

When she left the dining room Lucas was still sitting at the table, seemingly reluctant to end his interlude between problems. She set off to walk back to her flat, but at the top of St James's Street she suddenly felt weary, perhaps feeling burdened by Lucas and his problems, perhaps as a result of eating an unusually large breakfast. She turned left and entered Green Park tube. She did not much care for the tube. It was correctly named the underground. By a trick of the wind the smell of newly-cut grass in the park above had penetrated to the foot of the escalator. Imagine, Helen thought, if she were trapped below for some reason, because a bomb had exploded over London, or, more likely, because something had gone wrong with the tube; such a circumstance would make the longing to get to the surface almost unbearable. She had once read a story about people having to live underground, and being allowed to see what remained of the grass and trees only once a year, unless they were important.

She got out at Oxford Circus. The station's busker was producing some extraordinarily sweet music. When he came into view she saw he was playing a harp. Helen wondered how he had got it through the ticket gates. She put ten pence into his hat. Giving beggars a token coin was a ritual she practised based on her belief that no one should go though the humiliation of asking and being refused. At street level she no longer felt tired and she strode home. There was a letter on the mat. Official envelope, posted free. Helen disciplined herself not to tear it open and found a knife to slit it open neatly.

It contained a note from Jenkins, reminding her that the second part of her sergeant's exam was close, and would she like to talk to him about it? It seemed a kindly offer, but Helen wondered how much kindness there was in it. Ripley had made her suspicious of her superiors. Jenkins was a clubby sort. He could easily be a member of The Cause. All the same, his note was a reminder that she had better do some work. She needed a retreat, cut off from distractions, from temptations. A cell in a nunnery would do very well. This being difficult to arrange at short notice, she booked herself a room at the Royal Automobile Club and moved in with two pieces of luggage, a light one containing a change of clothing and a heavy one containing books. She emptied a space in her brain and packed it with material to gratify examiners, after which it could be disposed of.

After two days of study she allowed herself a walk in St James's Park. She sat on the grass and picked a strand and sucked at it, absorbing a few atoms of caesium 137. The grass was damp. Helen moved to a deckchair, one of hundreds, nearly all of them empty, put out by a park employee carried away by the early lilt of the day. Nearby, a woman and some friends were having a small celebration, presumably for her birthday. They had a cake with candles, which she had some difficulty lighting. Having done so, she blew them out to a cheer from her friends. Someone from the party came over to Helen, carrying a small piece of cake on a tissue.

'Will you join us?' Helen took the morsel. It had a dry taste.

'Delicious,' she said. 'Thanks, but I have to get back.' It was the first conversation she had had for two days. When she returned to her room the phone was ringing.

'At last I've tracked you down.'

'What is it Johnny?'

'I thought you would have heard.'

'He's dead?'

THIRTY-ONE

A long pause.
'Johnny?'
'Where have you been? Ripley has been killed. Murdered.'
'Oh, I see,' said Helen, who did not.
'Don't you read the papers? The *Guardian*, yesterday.'
'I've been cut off for a bit. Swotting. Can you give me the headlines?'
The mutilated body of an American soldier had been found on a beach in Little Cayman. The name tag on his uniform had identified him as Ripley. He was believed to hold the rank of a two-star general. American authorities said that at this stage they were unable to confirm the identification. An investigation was ongoing. Police sources on the island said there had been a wave of anti-Americanism as a result of the war in Iraq.
'So it may not be Ripley?'
'Has all that swotting made you dumb or something?'
'I suppose it is pretty clear? You seem to know all about it.'
'I know what my brain tells me. Ripley has been murdered. And not for some anti-Americanism. You can forget that nonsense.'
'I thought it was Lucas you were going to say.'
'He had better watch out.'
'You think he had something to do with this?'

'Something to do with this?' Johnny mimicked her voice. 'I suppose I am talking to Helen Berlin, a normally intelligent member of the police?'

'Don't get irritated, Johnny. I am just catching up. Lucas arranged for Ripley to be killed in Cayman?'

'Bright girl.'

Helen was herself again. Ripley dead. She remembered something that Lucas had said: he had made Ripley rich, 'for now'. Deadly words. Helen found herself laughing. The laughter of the absurd. The executioner sent to his own execution. The cruelty of it. Pure Ionesco.

'Sorry,' she said. 'I'm appalled really. But Ripley was corrupt.'

'The Americans don't like their people killed, even the corrupt ones.'

'So now the heat is on Lucas?'

'It has been on him ever since he came to London. He was slow to feel it.'

'Where is he now?'

A long pause.

'You can tell me, Johnny.'

'I was just trying to make an educated guess. Minsk, I would say. Possibly Smolensk. It depends at what time their coach crossed the border. There was some delay, I believe. The coach left London without Cathy the nanny. Her mother would not let her go. But in the end they flew to Warsaw and picked up the coach there.'

'Both of them?'

'So it seems.'

'And the others?'

'Robinson, and the TV chap. Daugava. That fellow from the Foreign Office, Carruthers something. A couple of drivers.'

'Are they all mad?'

'Not necessarily. I thought of going myself. All expenses paid. The best hotels. Your Lucas is a persuasive fellow.'

Her Lucas? As Helen put the phone down she felt abandoned, and felt foolish in feeling so.

THIRTY-TWO

It came by special delivery, a package the size of a shoe box. Helen signed for it on a form that was in Cyrillic as well as English. She held the package to her ear. She felt cautious. But would the absence of a tick mean that the contents were safe? Probably not; that was the stuff of comic books. The package was well sealed. Helen unwrapped layer after layer. The thought came to her of the children's game of pass the parcel. At the heart of the package was a small leather-covered box, and inside the box there glowed a black pearl.